SILENT SLIPPER

A JULIA FAIRCHILD MYSTERY

PJ PETERSON

FINNGIRL, LLC

Paperback ISBN: 978-1-957127-03-3

eBook ISBN: 978-1-957127-02-6

Published by:

Finngirl, LLC

PO Box 1563

Longview, WA 98632

Visit the author's website: www.pjpetersonauthor.com

This is a work of fiction. Names, characters, businesses, places, long-standing institutions, agencies, public offices, events, locales and incidents are either the products of the author's imagination or have been used in a fictitious manner.

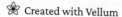

ALSO BY PJ PETERSON

Blind Fish Don't Talk

Rembrandt Rides a Bike

Pickled Pink in Paris

One Will Too Many

CHAPTER
ONE

Deep in the forest, the only sound was the steady beat of the native drums.

All of nature was reverently silent as the men and women in colorful sarongs moved sinuously around the young woman. She knelt, with her head bowed down, on a cushion of palm fronds in the center of the circle. The drummers punctuated the rhythm as the dancers swayed in time to the beat. Once they completed the third revolution, the drumming stopped.

The High Priest, wearing a tunic of finely tanned leather, and the Shaman, dressed in crude animal skins, stepped into the circle and bid the girl to raise her head. The High Priest bowed and handed a small pouch to the Shaman, the direct descendant of the ancestral great Shaman, and stepped back.

The Shaman raised the bag for all to behold, then ceremoniously turned away from the girl to face the dancers and other tribe members. After softly whispering a chant over the pouch, he reached in and produced a silver pendant, simple in style but finely crafted. The Shaman slowly turned in a circle with his hands raised, holding the necklace for all to see.

As the Shaman approached the girl, she stood and turned her back to him. He placed the necklace around her neck, being careful to secure the delicate clasp. The High Priest stepped forward to face the girl and made a sign with his hands. He recited an ancient chant, after which the girl responded with a nod. The High Priest then asked the girl to face the tribe. The tribespeople chanted an approval.

Thus, the traditional ceremony was finished, and a new shaman had been declared. The drumming resumed, much softer than before, slowly fading to an inaudible pulse as the circle of dancers dispersed into the tropical forest. Slowly, the life sounds of the tropical forest resumed their natural levels.

∽

SPANISH TOWN, Virgin Gorda

"Getting here reminds me of a line from a song—something about 'trains and boats and planes,'" said Julia.

"I hope we don't have to get on a train," said her sister Carly. "I seriously doubt they have one on this small island anyway. Taking three planes and the island ferry from St. Thomas was enough for me."

Julia smiled. It had been a long day made longer by a flight delay on the last leg from San Juan to St. Thomas. "At least we didn't miss this ferry ride. I was seriously sweating that final late departure getting here. This is the last ferry of the day into Virgin Gorda."

"One of us has good karma, fortunately," said Carly, smirking at her sister. "Who did you say is meeting us here?"

"Antonio, I believe, or his wife, Rita. The email said it depended on his work schedule."

The sisters pulled their carry-on luggage down the ramp to a concrete pier, where most everyone either walked to an adjacent parking lot and got into a car or were greeted by someone with a hug and kiss. There didn't seem to be anyone left over who could be either of their bed-and-breakfast hosts.

Carly turned to her slightly older sister and sighed loudly. "You were saying? Are you sure about the plan for picking us up?"

Julia groaned and pulled out her phone to check the details. Her eyes lit up and she nodded. "I'm sure. Maybe we arrived a little early. Let's chill for a few minutes and wait. I see a bench over there."

"I'm impressed you actually got here with a single carry-on, Julia. I had my doubts when you said you could do it, even though it was a great idea."

"'O ye of little faith,'" she said, scoffing. "Basically, I hate dealing with lost luggage, and there's always that chance, especially with two plane transfers along the way. Besides, we didn't have to pack half a dozen costumes this trip."

"And two or three sets of tap and jazz shoes. Do we have a schedule for the week? Or will this be a real vacation like you promised?"

Julia cringed. Their last girls' vacation in Paris had turned into a detective story when Julia and Carly had helped the Paris gendarmes find a murderer to keep Julia's long-distance beau, Josh, out of jail. "We will be footloose and fancy-free here. At least that's my plan."

"Miss Fairchild? Miss Pedersen?" A nice-looking man with dark, gray-tinged hair and a beautiful smile approached them. "I am Antonio. Welcome to Virgin Gorda."

Julia turned to Carly. "And the fun begins."

~

Saturday

"'Come with me to Virgin Gorda,' she said. 'It'll be fun,' she said." Carly dropped her daypack, plopped down on a boulder, and wiped her brow with a damp bandana. "What's so special about this beach anyway?" she asked as she pulled out her water bottle. "The heat here is suffocating. I need one of those proverbial trade winds right now."

Julia scanned the horizon, then checked the local tourist map, noting the visible landmarks. She admitted to herself, though not aloud to Carly, that the heat did feel rather miserable, especially compared to their normally cool and moist Pacific Northwest. "We're getting closer. Antonio said it was well worth the walk because it's less crowded than some of the other beaches. He said we might even find some sea glass."

"What's so special about sea glass? I've never heard of it."

Julia sighed dreamily. "A few years back I read a book about a young girl who was married but spent most of her time alone because her husband was gone a lot on a fishing boat. They lived on the coast somewhere in New England. Anyway, she took long walks along the beach and picked up the pretty pieces of glass that she found."

"Okay, but what *is* it?"

"I was getting to that. Sea glass is created from ordinary glass that has been in the water for a long time, like from broken bottles on ships. It changes color to soft greens and blues as it's polished by the water and sand. I'm not sure why that intrigues me, but I like to look for it. When I visited my friend Judy in Los Gatos last time, we found some when we were beachcombing at Santa Cruz. We even met a young lady who was collecting it to use in jewelry-making. I ended up giving most of mine to her, because she had a small child and a dog with her. I thought it might be her only source of income."

"That was nice of you."

"Thank you. I still wanted some to keep for myself, so we

went back the next day and found a little more. That's what's in the vintage cut glass bowl in my kitchen window."

"So that's what those rocks are. I wondered when I saw them last time I was at your house. Back to looking for the beach here. Are you sure we're heading to the right one?" Carly guzzled again from her bottle, then stood and struck a theatrical pose with her hand to her ear. "Hark! I hear the ocean now and it's not very far away."

Julia pretended to punch her silly sister, then joined Carly as they trudged their way farther down the trail through the dry, Caribbean terrain. A hundred yards farther, Carly stopped and held out her arm. "Wait."

"Do you see something? Are we there?" Julia stepped past her sister to see for herself. She glimpsed the tranquil water of the Caribbean Sea straight ahead. "There it is! It's beautiful. I love that turquoise color." She snapped a few photos for her expanding collection of travel pictures.

"But what about *that?*" Carly pointed off to the right. "I hope that's not a ... person."

Julia slinked up to a large boulder with something strewn across it. Flies buzzed around a body lying on top of a huge, flat rock. "Oh, no!" She didn't need her medical degree to know this woman was dead.

"Julia, what do we do?"

Already Julia was fumbling through her beach bag. "No cell service here," Julia said, after checking her phone. "Well, let's document what we found to give to the authorities." She took photos of the body from several angles. The small woman had long dark hair and was mostly clad, but her clothing was torn. She was barefoot. "This looks like a costume of some kind, maybe for a performance or dance. I don't think she's older than her late teens." Julia sighed. "It breaks my heart when young people die. Did you know that's why I didn't go into pediatrics?"

"I understand. I love kids, but I'm sure it's hard to take care of little ones with awful diseases like cancer. I don't know how pediatricians do what they do." Carly reached out to pat her sister on the arm. "Anyway, her dress reminds me of the harem girl costumes we wore when we performed that dance from *Aladdin*. She even has one of those jewels on her forehead." She shook her head sadly. "I'll look for her shoes."

Julia scanned the immediate area for anything that might belong to the young woman. She caught a flash of something shiny a couple of feet away, mostly hidden by the thick foliage. A small, silver pendant on a fragile chain shone in the sunlight. She used a tissue to pluck it from the base of the aloe-like shrub. She held it up and let it dangle in front of her face to determine what it might be. It had a dark red gemstone on the front with what looked like a religious image of some kind on the back, though she didn't recognize the saint it depicted.

"Hey, look at this. I'm pretty sure it's not Saint Christopher. I wonder who it is. The pendant is heavier than the medallions I saw in Rome a few years back. It also has an inscription on the back." She squinted but couldn't make out the minuscule lettering. "I don't think it's Latin. Maybe it's a native language." She took several photos, thinking that there was probably a Catholic Church in Spanish Town with a priest who might be able to identify it.

Carly emerged from behind a short palm tree with gigantic fronds and peeked at it. "I don't have a clue. Maybe it represents someone special to the local people." She motioned for Julia to follow her and pointed to a small slipper that was almost hidden under the scrub. "I didn't touch it. I knew better."

Julia took several photos at different angles before using

another tissue to retrieve the silver slipper. The dainty shoe had a curled-up toe and reminded Julia of footwear from Arabia or the Far East. She sighed as she carefully placed it, along with the pendant, in the side pocket of her pack and zipped it closed. "Too bad this slipper can't tell us what happened."

Carly said, "Well, so much for a fun day at the beach." She picked up her gear for the trek back.

"We'll need to find the police station in town and report this so they can pick up our Jane Doe," said Julia.

"Could you tell how long she might have been on that rock?"

"I'm not very good at estimating time of death, but I'm guessing she likely died within the past twenty-four hours. I didn't see evidence of major deterioration, which would almost certainly happen a lot faster here with this heat."

The sisters were unusually quiet as they retraced their steps to the trailhead, where they mounted the scooters they had borrowed from their host.

As THEY WALKED BACK, Julia strode ahead and began second-guessing her trip with her sister, knowing she had promised Carly that this would be their own special fun time. She certainly hadn't intended for them to get involved in anything somber. After all, Julia Fairchild, M.D., and her younger sister Carly Pedersen had traveled to Virgin Gorda purely for a vacation. Julia had promised to treat Carly to a girls-only trip after previous misadventures in Amsterdam and Paris. She had arranged a stay in a bed-and-breakfast with a lovely host couple who lived on the southwest side of the island, not far from Spanish Town. Other than taking time to explore the beaches, doing a bit of snorkeling and going on a few hikes, their time was absolutely unscheduled.

For Julia, a popular, busy internist in a medium-sized town, having totally free time was surreal. Carly's job in the accounting office at a large paper mill had its own share of stress, like when it was time to make payroll every two weeks. Or tax time. Or when there were union negotiations with extra requests for reports. It hadn't taken much to persuade her to join her sister and get away.

They had grown up with two more sisters and two brothers on a small farm, but had lost sisters number one and three. Those losses served to bond Julia and Carly even more closely together. Carly had been Julia's favorite little sister since childhood. They now treasured the time they got to spend with each other as adults, a few adventures here and there notwithstanding.

Taller, with blue eyes and brunette hair, Julia had been single since a short marriage right out of college, and periodically swore off men. She knew that her life as a physician was intimidating for a lot of guys. When other women her age might take a vacation with their spouses, Julia looked forward to time away with her sister, but now, this unfortunate event.

Julia felt a hand slip into hers and she looked back. Carly was smiling at her, obviously recognizing what her sister was feeling. "Somehow I think Rob won't be surprised," she said, giving Julia a little nudge. Carly, with her golden hair and hazel eyes, was married to a sweet man, Rob, who worked as an electrician at the same mill as his wife. He was cool about fending for himself when the sisters went off for girl-time. He had become familiar with the unusual adventures the two sisters had. Julia couldn't help but smile at her sister's attempt to make her feel better.

A COUPLE OF HOURS LATER, just before two o'clock, Julia and Carly presented themselves at the police station in Spanish Town. Once Julia had explained the reason for their visit, they were immediately ushered into the office of the chief of police. A large ceiling fan rotated slowly, pushing the warm air gently around the room. The windows were open to the outside but had heavy iron grids keeping bad guys out (or in?). The air smelled stale in the smallish room, despite the moving air.

They sat in two uncomfortable metal chairs facing a massive wood desk and a wall of certificates in simple, black document frames. A tallish, slender man with a thick shock of dark hair and a mustache à la Tom Selleck entered through a second door at the rear of the room.

"Hello, ladies. My name is Magnus Hawke. I'm the police chief in this region of the island. And you are?"

"Julia Fairchild," said Julia, offering her hand. "And my sister Carly Pedersen," who did the same.

"Welcome to our island." He smiled and sat down in the well-worn leather chair behind the desk. "I understand you made a discovery earlier today."

"Here are photos that I took of a young lady near the beach where we hiked," said Julia, handing him her phone. "Unfortunately, she was dead, but probably not for very long." She explained the location and gave him the necklace and shoe. "We didn't find a second shoe."

He looked at the photos for a couple of minutes. "I see. I had my sergeant check the missing persons list before I came into the room. He said he didn't see anyone who would fit this description, but that isn't unusual. We find that families often wait an extra day, thinking their daughter stayed overnight with friends or something like that." He handed the phone to Julia and leaned back in the chair.

"What about the clothes she's wearing? It seemed unusual that she would be dressed in what looks like a costume," said Julia.

"I guess it would depend on when she disappeared. She could have been dressed this way on Friday night, for example, and just happened to be found on Monday, as you say."

Julia nodded. "Are you able to do DNA testing here?"

"Not locally. We would send the evidence to a lab in San Juan, Puerto Rico. But in all likelihood, someone will be filing a missing person report soon and then we will know who she is. We'll retrieve the remains and wait for the appropriate person to claim her." He smiled confidently, as if the conversation were concluded.

"And," Julia couldn't help but ask, "find out how she died?"

"Of course. I'll arrange for an autopsy. Things don't happen quickly here, however. There's probably a simple enough explanation; we don't get many murders."

He stood, signaling an end to the discussion. Julia shared the photos and her contact information with the desk sergeant before leaving the building.

"He didn't seem very upset about our finding a dead person," said Carly as they walked to their scooters.

"He was quite complacent. Maybe it's an everyday occurrence." Julia shrugged.

"I don't think so. He said murders were rare here."

"Well, we've done our citizen's duty. Let's check with Antonio and Rita and plan something for tomorrow."

∿

JULIA AND CARLY sat with their hosts on the palm-shaded patio overlooking the azure Caribbean waters. Tropical birds flitted through the trees and chattered loudly like a serenade of sorts as they finished the evening meal. Fragrant flowers of yellow and red bougainvillea and hibiscus added a colorful backdrop.

The house itself was on the small side, set on a large beachfront lot at the edge of a tropical forest. With trees on two sides of the patio, the house on a third, and the open side facing the water, it felt like they had their own slice of paradise. All the windows were open, shutters at the ready in case of a seasonal storm. Each room had a ceiling fan that moved the air to create refreshing island breezes.

"This fish is delicious! I'd love to know how you prepare it." Julia took another bite and sat back as she savored the flavors. "I love this fresh fruit salsa and the rice dish, too. I might have to take you back home with me!"

"We didn't learn anything like this at Le Cordon Bleu in Paris last year," said Carly. "My husband, Rob, would love this. He catches a lot of salmon and steelhead in the Columbia River."

Once everyone was finished with the meal, they chatted and watched the sun slowly sink into the water. The birds fell silent almost immediately as the sky started to darken.

"I'm always amazed at how short the twilight is in the Caribbean. Hawaii, too," said Carly. "At home in the Pacific Northwest, it doesn't get dark for at least another hour after the sun goes down in the summer."

Antonio nodded. "Yes, the sun goes down quickly but we can sit out here in the dim light and have a cocktail while I play my guitar and enjoy the peace and quiet of the evening."

"Especially after those birds settle down," said Julia. "Is it my imagination or did they get louder just before sunset?"

Rita laughed. "I think they are telling each other all the hot bird news just before they go to sleep. They'll be chattering again just before sun-up tomorrow."

"Like the early edition of news on local television back home," said Julia. "Speaking of news, we need to tell you about finding a young girl at Savannah Bay today." She launched into a short version of finding the girl, then visiting the police station and the priest.

"Oh, how sad," said Rita. "I hate hearing stories like that."

The room was quiet, almost reverent, for a few minutes. Rita seemed especially somber, then she brightened a bit. "Let me refresh those drinks," she said, rising to pour wine from the decanter.

"You mentioned wanting some ideas for tomorrow," said Antonio. "I would suggest going to the copper mine on the other side of the island. The view from there is fantastic in every direction. It's easy to get there on the motorbikes." He sketched a map on his napkin. "If you go in the morning, you can spend the rest of the day at one of the beaches not far from there."

"Do you promise we won't find another body?" asked Carly.

Antonio chuckled. "Just stay away from Dead Chest Island."

Carly's eyes opened wide and Rita laughed. "That is simply the name of one of the small islands, my dear. You will love visiting the other side of this island, and I promise you'll have a great day."

CHAPTER

TWO

"This is a fabulous view. I can see for miles and miles. Or is it kilometers here? Anyway, Antonio's recommendation to check this out was right on," said Julia. She scanned the vast horizon from her perch on the remains of the wall of the abandoned mine high above the Atlantic Ocean below.

She and Carly had made their way to the old copper mine on the southeast corner of the island. They stood on the highest point of what was left of the original structure. The mine itself had been constructed in 1837 after the British Virgin Islands had gone under British rule. Spaniards passing through the British Virgin Islands were the first Europeans to mine copper here in the early eighteenth century. Later, following a decline in mineral deposits in Cornwall, England, Cornish miners built what remains as ruins today. Well before the Cornish and Spanish miners arrived, however, Amerindians used the copper to make tools and jewelry, which they traded with the indigenous people from other islands.

During the twenty-five years or so of operation, copper

was mined by thirty-six Cornish miners and about 140 British Virgin Islands workmen. They sent the ore along Copper Mine Road, which had been built for this purpose by the miners, to Spanish Town for shipment to Wales. Although the mine had been abandoned in 1862, parts of the original stack, the engine house, and the main building remained for curious visitors and history fans. At one time the shafts extended to a depth of forty fathoms (240 feet), partially under the sea. Several of the Cornish miners started families with native women and some of those descendants live in the islands today.

"It's interesting that the water is so different on the eastern side of Virgin Gorda compared to the Caribbean water on the west. The Atlantic Ocean swirls and snarls and looks angry even on a calm, sunny day like today."

"I wonder how many shipwrecks there were in the old days," said Carly.

"Are you thinking of the days of pirates and buried treasure? We could ask Antonio if there are any places on the island to look for pirate booty." Julia winked at her sister.

"I would think that thousands of people have already searched every square inch of the island. What could possibly be left to find?" Carly scrambled over the rubble along the ridge in search of a better vantage point.

Julia scanned the water with the binoculars she'd borrowed from their host. "That's interesting," she said as she handed them to Carly. "Look to the northeast, not far from shore."

Carly dutifully followed instructions. "Is that a Jolly Roger flag I'm seeing? That looks like a pirate ship. Just like in the movies."

"I think so, too. And we were just talking about pirates as if they were from a previous century."

"They were. At least I think they were."

"Today's pirates are a different breed. I still shudder when I remember being a prisoner on that yacht when I went to St. Maarten a couple of years ago."

Julia took the binoculars from Carly and searched the beach area nearest the ship. "I see some activity on land. There are a couple of SUVs and some people moving around. I wonder if they're all connected to that ship."

"Maybe they're shooting a movie and need some extras. I'd do it for free." Carly brushed her honey-blond curls out of her eyes as the salty air blew gently from the east.

"Antonio might know if that's the case. Or we could drive up that way and check it out ourselves," said Julia with a sideways look.

"What are we waiting for?" Carly grinned and led the way to where they'd left the scooters.

WITH THE HELP of a detailed island map courtesy of Antonio and the phone's GPS, they found the road that led to the beach they'd seen from the copper mine. Several large, nondescript vans, half a dozen SUVs, and a couple of movie cameras on mobile carts lined the narrow drive to the sandy oasis. Julia and Carly parked their scooters in the shade of the palm trees and walked toward the people gathered in clusters on the beach.

A couple of pirates wearing traditional shirts with long sleeves and ruffles under long, tan coats with big, silver buttons lounged in beach chairs. Black tricorn hats had been tossed onto a nearby table. Julia assumed the two men were acting as captains in the movie. Maybe one was the understudy, she thought when she realized they were dressed identically. Other men wore ragged striped shirts of various hues, loose pants, and sported colorful bandanas wrapped around their heads. Scattered on the set she saw coolers filled with ice and water bottles.

"Miss! Miss!" Julia heard a stern male voice yelling from behind her. She turned to see a stubby man with longish brown hair and a round, red face moving her way, breathing heavily as he did so.

When he got within ten feet of her, he said, "This is a private area. You aren't allowed here."

"Hello, sir. My sister and I saw the ship on the water and wondered if you were shooting a movie," said Julia, pointing to the obvious pirate ship off to the right.

"Yes, that's why you can't be here. Thank you for your interest and you can leave now." His voice was high-pitched and whiny.

"We can't stay and watch? We won't get in the way." Julia smiled politely and stood her ground.

"Do you need any extras?" Carly smiled that pheromone-charged grin of hers.

The man, whom they assumed was the director of the movie, smiled reflexively and relaxed his shoulders. Carly did have a way with men. "Not today, but I suppose you can stay and watch for a while. Stand by that striped cabana, please." He pointed toward the palm-shaded area where several tents had been erected, one of them being the blue-and-white-striped cabana. "I'm Brock Hughes, the director." He extended a hand and shook both Julia's and Carly's hands. "Sorry I was grumpy. We've had a bunch of rowdy teenagers hanging around almost every day and we're behind on our schedule."

"Thank you. We'll be very quiet and stay out of your way," promised Julia.

The sisters strolled toward the row of white tents that lined the beach. The first one they passed was being used to apply makeup. Trays of cosmetics lined two small tables on the far side, where a young woman and man sat in tall chairs talking to each other. They looked up when they noticed Julia and Carly in the doorway. "Hi. Are you here for your makeup?" asked the young guy with blue eyes and sandy hair. Julia thought he could be in movies himself.

Carly blushed and giggled. "No, not us. We're just visiting the set."

"I'm Matt," he said, rising and offering his hand, "and my partner is Lissa." She had long, chestnut hair with gold highlights and multiple small earrings lining each ear. And a nose ring. She nodded but stayed in her chair. "We have time if you want to give it a try."

"Thanks. Maybe later." Carly's face was still pink as she and Julia waved goodbye.

"I can't believe you turned Matt down. What fun it would be to be made up like a movie star." Julia slinked like a model on the red carpet as she walked through the sand.

Carly grinned. "I was tempted. But Brock said we're supposed to stay by the other tent."

The next tent along the way contained several racks of clothing and shelves of boots and shoes. It looked like typical pirate wardrobe stock.

In the third tent, they saw similar racks, but the clothing and shoes appeared to be for women.

"I didn't notice any women on the set, Julia. Did you?"

"There must not be scenes for them today but ... look at this ..." Julia did a double-take when she noticed the shoes. "Isn't that the same kind of silver shoe we found yesterday?" She pointed to a pair of silver slippers with turned-up toes.

"Yes, and those dark pink kimono-like dresses look like the one that girl was wearing." Carly held her hand over her mouth.

"Do you suppose she's an actress connected to this movie?" Julia whispered, suddenly aware that they could be overheard. "And if she is, do we talk to the director or go to Chief Hawke?"

"Julia, we go to the police. We are on vacation. You are not detecting this time. *You promised.*" Carly glared at her sister, hands on her hips, foot tapping rapidly on the sand.

"Spoilsport. Okay. I know you're right. Let's spy—I mean, observe—from the cabana for a while. Then we can tell Chief Hawke what we found here. It'll be up to him to follow up on it."

Julia and Carly finally moved to the blue-and-white-striped cabana and stood in the shade. They had a good view of the beach set and watched the shooting for a while. The director, Brock, yelled "Shoot" and "Cut" half a dozen times for every few minutes of acting, reshooting each scene several times. Two pirates were burying small chests in the sand while three others stood guard. Julia assumed they were supposed to be standing sentry and watching for the people who would have lived on the island in the era being depicted.

During a lull in the acting, one of the pirate captains sauntered toward the sisters and grabbed a bottle of water from a cooler near them. He had, Julia noticed, walked past several other coolers on his way. He sidled up to Carly and asked, "Which part are you playing?"

"Innocent bystander," she replied.

He cocked his head. "Huh? I didn't know that was one of the roles."

Carly smiled effervescently. "It's not. My sister and I are watching as guests. Your director said we could stay for a while."

"Well then, I'm Noah." He did a small bow. "And you are?"

"Carly. And Julia." She pointed to her sister. "She's Julia." They shook hands all around.

He winked at Carly. "You could be in the movies. I think there are a couple of scenes in which Brock needs extras."

Carly blushed again and shook her head. "Not me. I can't perform in public. And he said he didn't need extras."

"It's not performing, honey. It's all an act." He finished guzzling his water, then turned toward the beach. "Time to play my part. See ya." He saluted as he walked back to the set. He turned one last time, winked, and said, "Don't forget. Noah Langdon."

THREE

"We should go to the police station and at least tell Magnus—I mean Chief Hawke—what we saw," said Julia as they walked back to the scooters. "It'll be up to him to decide whether or not to investigate whether those costumes are the same as the dead girl's clothes and shoes."

"It's Sunday. We could call him and save ourselves the time and travel. He's probably at home anyway."

"That'll work. Hey, I'm hungry. Do you want to check out the café in Spanish Town that Rita mentioned?"

The Sapphire Lighthouse Bar was popular with locals and tourists alike, according to Rita. Inside the tropical-themed restaurant and bar, Julia and Carly saw gigantic, slow-moving fans on the ceilings, windows open to the ocean breeze, and multiple small, high-top tables filled with customers. They wandered to the outdoor patio and found a table with a view of the water and a small sliver of beach. Julia took in a lungful of the fresh ocean air and sat down on an iron-backed bistro chair as Carly followed suit. A bronze-skinned girl with long, black hair and dressed in a colorful tropical pareo and matching top appeared at the table with tall glasses of ice water. She had an electric smile and perfect white teeth.

"How may I help you?" she asked with a slight accent that to Julia's ears was hard to pinpoint.

Julia smiled and said, "Thank you. We'd love to start with iced tea."

After perusing the lunch menus, Julia said, "This is heavenly!" She felt her shoulders relax as she gazed at the water. "The temperature here is perfect. Antonio said it rarely gets too hot or too cold. And with a slight breeze today it is perfect. Seems too good to be true."

"Our Washington weather is like that—not too hot or too cold most of the time."

"But are you forgetting our wet fall weather and our rainy springs?"

Carly chuckled. "I'm just agreeing that it's rarely too hot or too cold. I was ignoring the wet aspect. This food all sounds yummy. I'm going to try the shrimp salad with mango-lime dressing."

"I'll try the panko-crusted fish if you let me taste your coconut shrimp."

The sisters enjoyed the perfectly prepared food in the lazy afternoon ambiance of the café. Julia was tempted to lick her fingers and Carly pretended to lick her plate but giggled instead when she noticed Julia's glare. Afterward, they lounged in comfortable rattan chairs at the edge of the patio with glasses of chilled pinot grigio to finish their meal. The sun on Julia's face disappeared for a moment. When she opened her eyes, she saw the handsome face of Noah Langdon peering at her.

"Fancy meeting the two of you here," he said. "May I join you?" He held a frosted glass of beer in one hand and with the other twirled a chair around to join them, their agreement already assumed.

"We'd love it," said Julia. She noticed Carly unconsciously fluffing her hair.

Noah straddled the bistro chair, resting his arms across the back. He now wore light-colored chinos and a short-sleeved white linen shirt. A bit of dark chest hair peeked out from the open neck. He was devastatingly handsome. "I didn't catch your names earlier. I'm still Noah."

Julia offered her hand after wiping it dry on her sundress. "I'm Julia. That's my sister Carly."

Noah took both girls' hands at the same time. "I can't believe my good luck finding you here. Are you locals?"

Julia shook her head. "Tourists. Vacationing here for the week."

"It's wet and cold in February back home," said Carly. "We were just talking about the weather here compared to home. Washington state."

"Where's home for you?" asked Julia. "I thought I heard a bit of an accent that I didn't notice this morning."

"I grew up in Vermont but my mom's from Ireland so I have a blend of rural New England and Irish, I guess." He laughed. Even his laugh sounded special.

"I'm assuming you're done filming for the day," said Julia. "Those costumes must be hot out there in the sun."

"For sure. I don't know how the pirates of old wore all those clothes." Noah shook his head as he drank down his beer and signaled to the waitress for another one.

"Maybe they only wear them in the movies," said Carly. "I mean, does anyone know what they really dressed like in those days?"

Noah nodded. "That's what historical costume designers

are for. They do the research and we play the part dressed in whatever they've come up with."

"So are you done for the day?" asked Julia.

"For the day, yes, but we're going to do some more filming later this evening. Brock, the director, wants to do a scene of burying the treasure chests after dark. He figures it'll be more realistic." Noah made a face, suggesting he wasn't wild about the idea.

"Same place as this morning?" Carly finished her drink and sat up straighter. "Do you think we could watch again?"

"Probably. I don't think Brock really cares about visitors, except for the local boys. They keep trying to sneak into the wardrobe tent. I guess they want to pretend to be pirates." He rolled his eyes.

"What do you think, Julia?"

"Let's see if Antonio and Rita have anything planned. And we still have to call the police chief."

"Police? Why do you have to call the police?" Noah accepted his second glass of beer when the waitress arrived at his side. She lingered a moment longer than necessary before leaving, totally ignoring Julia's nearly empty glass. Noah, however, kept his eyes on the sisters as he drank half of his second glass down in two gulps.

Julia and Carly looked at each other. Julia gave Noah an abridged version of finding the body at Savannah Beach the day before. She left out the part about the costume-looking attire and silver shoe. "He said we could call today. We're hoping they have figured out whether she matches someone's missing family member."

"Of course." He glanced at his cell phone before saying, "Gotta run. My ride is on the way. Maybe I'll see you again this week." He gulped down the last of his beer and was gone after laying some money on a table where the waitress was taking another order.

"Did it seem to you that he was in a hurry after we mentioned the police?" Julia asked as she finished her drink and signaled the waitress.

"I thought so, too. Maybe he doesn't like to talk about dead bodies."

"I wonder if he changed his mind about having us show up for the buried treasure scene."

The waitress wouldn't accept their money. "The man paid for everything," she said with a beautiful smile. But she finally accepted a tip from Julia "for arranging the weather."

JULIA AND CARLY stopped by the police station in person since they were already in town. They were surprised that Police Chief Hawke was in the building, considering that it was a Sunday.

"I like to get a head start on Monday by coming in for a few hours on Sunday afternoons," he said when Julia asked about it. "It seems that we get as many calls on Friday night and Saturday as we do the rest of the week. My coming in on Sundays makes Monday morning a bit more pleasant, or maybe I should say less hectic. Come on into my office." For the next ten minutes, he listened attentively to their recitation of visiting the movie crew's site.

When they were done, he said, "Please call me Drew. My middle name is Andrew, thankfully. I don't know what my parents were thinking with a name like Magnus. It's too heavyweight for this island." He shook his head and smiled as he sat back in his well-worn leather chair. "So you two are thinking this young lady on the beach had something to do with the movie?" He stroked his beardless chin and cocked his head.

"Not necessarily," said Julia. "It just seemed curious that she was wearing clothes that were very similar to the costumes we saw in one of the tents."

"It's worth checking out. No one has reported anyone of her description missing as of today. I suppose she could be connected to this movie. I had assumed earlier that she was a local girl. I could be wrong."

Julia asked, "Has the cause of death been determined?"

Drew smiled. "Not yet. As I mentioned yesterday, such things tend to take time, especially on the island."

Julia nodded. "Noah, one of the actors, said they were done filming for the day but would be doing some beach scenes this evening."

"He didn't answer when I asked him if it would be at the same beach, though," said Carly, looking at her sister.

"That's true."

"They shouldn't be too difficult to find," said Drew. "Virgin Gorda is a small island and there are only so many beaches that can be reached with all that movie gear in tow." He stood, effectively dismissing them. "We'll take it from here."

"May I ask one more question, please?" Julia pulled up the photos of the girl and necklace. "Would it be all right if we ask the priest at the Catholic Church about the pendant, and see if he knows the young lady? I know it's a long shot, but I'd like to check it out."

Drew thought for a moment. "Yes, go ahead. And please report back to me whatever you find out."

~

"WE HAVE time to swing by the church and see if the priest can identify the pendant if he's there," said Julia once they were ready to leave on their scooters. "I checked the map, and we can be there in a few minutes."

"Works for me, although I think it should be a police matter."

"Drew said we could check it out. I would bet there are only a couple of policemen on the whole island, so it saves him some work. I admit I'm curious about the pendant for my own reasons. The image looks very primitive compared to other medallions I've seen."

It was a short ride to St. Ursula's Church, which had been built on a hill on the road to The Baths, a popular tourist attraction. The doors to the church itself were closed and locked so Julia and Carly poked around the outside of the small building, where they found an entrance to the parish office around the corner. They knocked, then stepped through the open door into a small office where they saw an elderly man dressed in ordinary slacks and shirt. The office seemed inviting despite its overall simplicity and austerity. Small paintings, wooden icons, and several large plants softened the look.

"How may I help you today?" the man asked, looking up from his work. He had a Bible open in front of him on the desk and had been writing something in the notepad to his right.

"Good afternoon, sir," said Julia. "We're hoping to talk with the priest, if he's still here, and ask him questions about a medallion we found yesterday. We thought it might have a saint on it."

"Well, then, you're in luck. I'm Father Lorenzo." He stood and offered his hand. "Please sit down. I was here working on next week's homily because I'll be out of the office for a couple of days this week and this is the only time I could find to write.

But it can wait. I'd love to hear about this medallion." He leaned forward, elbows on the desk, palms clasped.

"Thank you, Father." Julia showed the priest the pictures she'd taken. "I don't know all the saints by any means but this rendition seems quaint compared to what I saw when I was at the Vatican a few years back. And there's something written on the back. I couldn't guess the language at all."

Father Lorenzo studied the photos of the front and back of the pendant, and nodded as he returned the phone. He sat back in his wooden swivel chair, his hands crossed on his chest. "I'm quite sure that your pendant is very old, not modern at all. The saint is in the style that I've seen in books depicting icons of the fifteenth or sixteenth century."

"What about the writing?"

"It might be Portuguese. It's not Spanish or Latin, I'm sure. Where did you say you found this?"

"It was in the sand near Savannah Beach. Our host had suggested we go there because it's less crowded than some other popular beaches." Julia briefly described how they had seen the body first, then found the necklace nearby, as she scrolled back to the photos of the young woman. "Do you know her?"

Father Lorenzo made the sign of the cross as he studied the photos carefully before he gave the phone back to Julia. "I'm afraid she's not one of our regular parishioners. There are several other churches on the island that you can visit. Perhaps you'll have more success at one of them."

"Yes, Father," said Julia. "I was hoping she would be Catholic because of the pendant."

"She could still be Catholic, but not attending church," he replied. "That's the sad truth all around the world these days." He sat forward with his fingers laced together, elbows on the desk, as though he were making a church steeple with his hands.

"One more thing. Do you have a book with photos of fifteenth- or sixteenth-century icons?"

"Not here, but I'm sure there's one at the diocesan office in Basseterre on St. Kitts Island."

"Do you suppose you could send these photos to St. Kitts and see if someone there can compare this saint to pictures in their library?"

"What a delightful idea! Let's do just that."

For the next several minutes Julia busily forwarded the photos to the email address that Father Lorenzo provided.

"I can't promise instant results," he warned. "They have limited staff, mostly volunteers, and this will require hands-on searching. But if it will help you and the police find out more about this unfortunate young lady, I'm happy to add my personal plea for expediency."

FOUR

After a delicious meal of pizza topped with artichoke heart and black olives and a local draft beer at a nearby pub, The Bath and Turtle, Julia and Carly felt revived. The first two full days of their vacation had seemed much longer. They lingered at the table enjoying the glow of the sunset over the Caribbean water.

"Let's decide what we want to do tomorrow," said Julia. "We haven't had any beach time yet ..."

"Because we ran into a body and a movie crew," said Carly. "And we've used up two days already."

"I know. We can start over in the morning and enjoy a whole day of beach-combing and working on our suntans."

"Rita said we could use the snorkeling gear anytime we like."

"I'm sure we can find a quiet beach with good snorkeling." Julia unfolded the local map which listed the best beaches and a couple of brochures she'd picked up from the counter. "Or we could go on one of these day trips on a catamaran. This one includes lunch, rum punch, and two snorkeling spots."

"That sounds good. And we wouldn't have to worry about getting lost or having to walk to one of those beaches."

Julia nodded. "And it would probably be less crowded. The brochure says that this boat goes to beaches that are less accessible by land."

"Even better. Call them."

Reservations made for the next day, they walked to their scooters. "What do you think about stopping in at the movie set?" Julia asked as she straddled her bright blue machine. She glanced at Carly.

Carly looked at her sister with her brows furrowed. "Why? Is it that Noah guy?"

"No. It's not him. I think you're more his type anyway." She smiled. "I was thinking about the costumes. Maybe we'll get a chance to talk to one of the women and find out if anyone is missing."

"Julia! No detecting. You promised." Carly started her metallic red scooter's engine. "It's a police problem. Not yours."

Julia knew her sister was right but felt a responsibility to the young woman who still had no name as far as she knew. Finding answers to puzzles was in her DNA, although usually that meant solutions for her patients' medical complaints. "From what Noah said, it's probably just the men pirates who would be burying treasure anyway." She reluctantly started her own scooter and followed Carly on the road to their temporary home just as the sun was setting.

THE CIRCULAR DRIVEWAY in front of the pristine white bungalow reminded Julia of some of the mansions she'd seen when she lived in Dallas, where she had done her medical residency. A multi-level fountain surrounded by a short, manicured hedge stood in the center of the space. A pergola covered with fragrant jasmine stood at the front door. The heavenly aroma filled their noses as the sisters entered the home with its terra-cotta tile floor and white walls.

The sisters found Antonio and Rita outside on the patio. Julia found herself smiling at the sight of the handsome couple. Antonio looked every bit the middle-aged Italian gentleman, with a constant smile and happy eyes. His light-colored chinos and light blue shirt accentuated his good looks. Rita's bronzed skin, long, black hair and dark eyes fit in with the tropical setting, as did the simple sheath dresses she wore.

Antonio offered drinks once they were settled in comfort-able chairs. A water fountain at the edge of the patio gurgled happily. The sky by now was a deep blue and the stars twinkled in the inky darkness. "The constellations are all wrong here," said Julia, between sips of the delicious concoction that Antonio had called a Painkiller. The rum and juices blended perfectly with a sprinkling of nutmeg on top. "This is divine."

"It's a good thing I'm not counting calories this week," said Carly. "I could drink a lot of these."

Antonio laughed. "It's a popular drink here in the Virgin Islands. Sometimes I wonder if the constellations were named by people who drank too much rum."

"Those early Greeks and Romans probably didn't drink rum," said Julia. "But they certainly had great imaginations when it came to picking out bulls and virgins and other shapes in the night sky."

Carly giggled. "Like a modern-day dot-to-dot puzzle."

"I can pick out Orion most of the time and Pleiades and the Big Dipper. Then I get lost."

Antonio pointed out several constellations that were visible in the sky. "We can see the Big Dipper sometimes, but usually in the middle of the night when it is close to the horizon. But there is the Southern Cross." He pointed to the small group of stars that actually resembled its name, unlike many star clusters.

"Antonio, is there an antiquities or relics shop on the island?"

"Not exactly. Why do you ask?"

Julia told him about the necklace they'd found. On Saturday night they had told their landlords of their sad discovery of the girl's body but hadn't mentioned the pendant. "Father Lorenzo at St. Ursula's church mentioned that it looked like it could be from the fifteenth or sixteenth century. Pirate's treasure maybe?"

Antonio cocked his head. "Now and then someone finds a piece of gold or jewelry on the beach of one of our islands. A few years ago a woman found a cache of jewelry in the sand on a beach on Grand Cayman Island. But I haven't heard of anything found here recently." He turned to his wife and asked, "Rita, do you know of any jewelry found on the island?"

"Many years ago, but not anymore," she replied.

"Did Blackbeard the pirate really live here?" asked Carly. "Was he a real person or was he just made-up for stories?"

"He was very real, Carly. Blackbeard, whose real name was Edward Teach or Thatch, lived in Soper's Hole on Tortola for a few years. He turned to piracy sometime after Queen Anne's War ended in 1714, during which he had worked as a so-called 'privateer.' He used to lie in wait in the deep harbor at Soper's Hole, hidden from view of the shipping channel, and would wait for the Spanish treasure ships to come passing through. Legend has it that once he marooned fifteen men on Dead Chest Island across from Tortola. That's where the pirate song about 'Fifteen Men on a Dead Man's Chest' comes from. Robert

Louis Stevenson made up that little ditty when he wrote *Treasure Island.*"

"Really?" Carly tucked her legs under her as she listened intently to Antonio.

"Yes, really. Eventually, in a big storm, his ships ran aground off the coast of North Carolina. The shipwrecks were found in the 1990s. *Queen Anne's Revenge* was his flagship. They've recovered cannons, parts of the hull, tools, glass trading beads and much more. So, yeah, he was real."

"What about buried treasure? Or is that just a rumor?" asked Julia.

"As you can imagine, with about 150 shipwrecks in the area, much of any gold and other valuables is still sitting at the bottom of the sea, probably covered by sand from the movement of the water. Story has it that Blackbeard used Dead Chest Island for burying his gold and jewelry, but it might just be a story. Are you planning to do some digging?"

"No," Julia replied. "I was wondering about where the pendant may have come from. As in, did someone dig it up around here?"

"And that's why you asked about a relics shop, I assume."

"Yes. I suppose I could do an online search and find something in the states, like Miami."

"San Juan, Puerto Rico, would be a better bet," said Antonio. "The shops there are much more likely to have the information you want. They've been around for centuries."

JULIA AND CARLY hunkered down with Julia's laptop, grateful that their host had wi-fi, and did a search for antiquities shops in San Juan. It was harder than they'd expected to find a shop that dealt with relics several hundred years old. Julia selected a couple of promising sites and composed an inquiry letter to accompany her photos of the medallion. "Now all we can do is wait for an answer."

"I don't get why you care so much about identifying the saint," said Carly. She sat cross-legged on a chair and surveyed her toenails for chips, then dabbed fresh polish on the offending nails.

"It's not so much about the saint but the possibility that the necklace is an authentic relic from pirate days. What if we found out that it *is* a fifteenth- or sixteenth-century piece? Then the question would be how she came to be in possession of it."

"And that matters because ...?"

"Did she find it on the beach somewhere? Did someone else find it and give it to her? Is it stolen from a private collection?" Julia finished the second email and poured a glass of cabernet sauvignon for herself and Carly. "It matters to someone."

"I suppose. Antonio mentioned we should go to The Baths in the morning. He said there's usually a group of manta rays —he called it a 'squadron'— that hangs out near the beach and we can swim with them. I'd like to try that."

"Sounds interesting."

"He said going in the morning is best because the tourist boats start showing up by noon and then it gets really crowded and the water gets rougher, too, with the afternoon winds. And the boats scare off the fish."

Julia's phone rang. The number was a local code. She hesitated before answering it. Only the police officer had her cell number. "This is Julia."

"Hello, Dr. Fairchild. This is Officer Hawke. Drew. Is this a good time to talk?"

"Um ... yes. What's going on?" She mouthed the word

"police" to her sister. "I'm putting you on speaker. Carly's right here."

"Perfect. I got a call from the coroner at Peebles Hospital on Tortola where the pathologist performed the autopsy."

"Were you able to find the woman's family?"

"No, unfortunately. We don't have a name yet. But Dr. Sundberg identified a cause of death. She had excessive levels of both fentanyl and cocaine in her bloodstream. The pathologist said she most likely died from an overdose, causing respiratory collapse."

Julia furrowed her brows. "I didn't see physical stigmata of drug use when I briefly examined her. Did Dr. Sundberg find any?"

"He said he didn't see any needle tracks, if that is what you mean. So, she may not have been a regular IV drug user. Of course, she may have used drugs in tablet form. Here in the islands, we don't have a major drug problem amongst our own, but because of our beaches and coves, modern-day pirates use our island as a transfer point in their distribution system. One method they use is to recruit young people such as this young lady to move the drugs from one point to another. If they're at risk of being caught, they're instructed to swallow the packets of cocaine or fentanyl."

"I've seen that happen back home as well. As you well know, fentanyl is made cheaply in places such as Mexico and South America and transported to the drug trade in the United States," said Julia. "It's also used to make knockoffs of meds such as popular tranquilizers or pain meds. She may have thought, for example, that she was taking a legitimate medication but was getting a false version of it containing fentanyl instead. Unfortunately, unsuspecting users get unpredictable levels of the fentanyl, sometimes leading to death by accidental overdoses."

"That is *so* scary," said Carly. "It's almost a miracle that anyone survives being a teenager anymore, what with these drugs all around us and so many other temptations."

"That it is," said Drew with an audible sigh.

Julia asked, "Are you any closer to knowing her identity?"

"Not yet. We've released the photos to the other islands in the BVIs and to the American Virgin Islands. We hope that someone will know her."

"I sent pictures of the necklace to a few antiquities stores in San Juan. I thought if we could identify the saint and the inscription, it might help us learn who our little 'Jane Doe' really is. I hope that's okay." Julia had crossed her fingers since she hadn't asked specifically for permission to take that step.

"Good idea! It might not help but it couldn't hurt. But I suspect it will turn out to be a souvenir of some kind from another island. Let me know what you find out."

"Will do. Thank you, Drew."

Julia had no sooner hung up than she realized she'd forgotten to ask about the woman's costume and what they had found out from the movie crew. She didn't want to bother him, however, and obviously it must've been a dead-end since they still didn't know the girl's identity.

Carly was sorting through her suitcase for the swimsuit she knew she'd packed but hadn't found yet. With the elusive item in hand, she hooted triumphantly, then scowled and said, "I don't understand why she would willingly swallow drug packets—if that's what really happened. She could just throw them away or hide them somewhere."

"I'm sure she was told that bad things would happen to her family if she didn't cooperate. And was promised nice things if she did what was asked. She was no longer a free person once she was in their clutches. I suppose it's like young people who try to get out of gangs but can't once they've been marked."

"That's so sad," said Carly. "I didn't know about this side of the drug world."

"Most people don't." Julia smiled kindly. "Okay." She sat cross-legged on the bed. "What we know for the moment is that we've found a young woman wearing an unusual pendant and clothing that looked like carbon copies of the ones we saw in the costume tent, a pirate movie being filmed on the island, and evidence of drug trafficking. I wonder if they're all connected."

Carly raised a finger. "No detective work, sis. You promised."

"I'm just thinking."

"That's what always gets us in trouble."

CHAPTER
FIVE

The Caribbean sun streamed into the room Monday morning with a promise of another glorious day. Julia and Carly quickly dressed and gathered their gear—sunscreen, coverups, hats—for the excursion on the catamaran. Antonio had offered to give them a lift to the dock where they would board the fifty-foot catamaran for a half-day sail to Cooper Island with snorkeling at Cistern Rock. The brochure had indicated that on the return trip they would sail past The Baths, where granite boulders up to forty feet in diameter lined the white sand beach.

The thirty or so passengers staked out their favorite spots on the gleaming white boat. A few of the younger people were already tanned, maybe from pre-vacation tanning beds, thought Julia. Most of the crowd were older folks, many with pale, untanned skin. Julia hoped they had brought heavy-duty sunscreen to slather on during the journey.

Julia and Carly opted for a mid-boat perch in front of the cockpit. They settled in, wearing sunglasses and wide-brimmed hats for the two-hour journey to the small island southwest of Virgin Gorda. The gentle breeze was welcomed as the morning temperature was already in the high seventies.

The shimmering, turquoise water at their destination beckoned. The captain of the catamaran had anchored near a reef about 200 feet offshore. The guests quickly gathered their gear and soon were all slipping into the water. Julia enjoyed the delicious coolness as she slowly moved through the water, almost floating above the coral, flippers propelling her along the beautiful reef. She took note of the many different colors, shapes and sizes of the tropical fish, which seemed to be in greater numbers than she recalled seeing on a Hawaii snorkeling outing several years earlier.

She felt a tap on her leg and turned her head to see that Carly had signaled her to stop for a minute.

"Wow," said Carly. "Now I can see why you wanted to snorkel here." She had taken her mask off for a moment and cleared her nose of saltwater. "And the water is a perfect temperature. No wetsuit needed. This is heavenly."

"I'm glad we get to enjoy a day like this," said Julia.

After about thirty minutes they made their way back to the boat and ate the snack provided. Fruit and nuts with local cheese and crackers accompanied by chilled pinot grigio, even in a plastic glass, were as good as fine dining after the refreshing physical activity.

The second snorkeling stop was on the way back to Spanish Town. The captain anchored the catamaran near a reef and announced they would have thirty minutes for exploring. Julia and Carly slipped into the refreshing water again, eager to maximize their time in the Caribbean water.

"Did you see that barracuda hanging out near the anchor?" Carly asked Julia as they removed their fins and masks once they were back on the boat. "I moved as fast as I could when I saw him."

Julia laughed. "I've been told they're not likely to attack humans unless they feel threatened. I gave him a wide berth."

"That was amazing. I lost track of how many different species of fish and coral I saw. I'm really glad we did this today."

"Same here. Now we can relax and enjoy lying in the sun for the rest of the way back to the dock." Julia took in a lungful of air.

The remainder of the cruise was relaxing. Some people managed to sleep as the boat sailed on, but Julia and Carly were still invigorated from the morning's snorkel.

About halfway back to Virgin Gorda, Julia poked her sister, whose eyes were closed. "Carly. Look to the right. There's another one of those pirate ships."

"Yeah. So what?"

"Last time we saw it, it was sailing on the other side of Tortola. I wonder if it's a different ship. Can you tell?"

Carly sat up and inspected the boat, which was not very far away from them. "I don't remember any red paint on the last one we saw. It could be a different one, I suppose."

"So that's at least two of them. I wonder why this one is on this route. It doesn't seem logical for a day sail from San Juan."

"You're probably reading too much into it." Carly lay back down and closed her eyes again.

Another fifteen minutes passed in silence. Julia's mind wandered from pirate ships to Chinese concubines to movies. As they approached the southern end of Virgin Gorda, she nudged her sister again.

"Look, Carly. Those boulders at The Baths are amazing! I'd love to go there and get a closer look."

"Maybe we can do that this afternoon," said Carly. She added with a snarl, "Unless you have sleuthing on your agenda."

WITH A FREE AFTERNOON and still waiting for information from the antiquities shop and the diocesan office, the sisters grabbed the scooters and headed to The Baths with its white sand.

Rita had packed a picnic snack for them to enjoy. She had told them the eating places near their destination were both expensive and very crowded during the day.

The road to the beach was well marked with little traffic, perhaps because it was a weekday. Slathered again with sunscreen and wearing their wide-brimmed straw hats, the sisters walked the short distance to the beach and staked out a prime spot.

"This place is like heaven—beautiful aquamarine water, white sand and a gentle breeze," said Julia, sitting on her towel and hugging her knees.

"Not to mention there are no crowds, and we also have a lovely view of islands in the distance." Carly did a pirouette in the sand before joining Julia on the beach towel big enough for two. "I'm glad we came over here. I'm ready to start reading that new book by Gary McAvoy you told me about. Father Dominic sounds dreamy, from what you said."

"It's not a romance. You know I don't read those. Give me a good mystery any day. Anyway, the main character is a priest. And he works for the Vatican and solves mysteries."

"I can have my fantasies if I want." She opened the book and sighed dramatically as though she were getting ready to read a steamy novel.

Julia shook her head and pulled out her own reading material: a draft of proposed bylaws for the corporation that managed the historic 1925 theater in her hometown. She had joined the board of directors a couple of years earlier and was on the committee that was charged with revising the outdated document. She would rather read a good mystery, but this needed to be done and she didn't think it would take long to review.

Carly tapped her arm. "Do you see what I see? Look toward the left."

Julia followed Carly's finger and saw a pirate ship coming from the southwest side of the island. "That's not the same one we saw this morning. There's no red on the trim. That's gotta be our friends Brock and Noah. I wonder where they're headed."

"It looks like they're sailing toward Tortola. Maybe they're filming on another island today." Carly turned to Julia and asked, "Do you think all the cast members travel on the ship?"

Julia shook her head. "I doubt it. They probably move by ferry or a chartered boat of some kind. There's probably a real sailing crew on board that moves the ship from place to place. Like the replica of *The Lady Grey* that I've seen in Astoria. The average person, let alone an actor, wouldn't know how to manage a square-rigger."

"You're probably right. It would make more sense."

"Uh-oh," said Julia. "Look to the left of the pirate ship. That catamaran is probably coming into this beach. With a lot of people on board."

"Let's check out those humongous boulders quickly before they get on shore and then we can go to the other beach around the corner. It'll be quieter there, I hope."

The sisters climbed through the gigantic granite rocks and hidden pools that composed The Baths. The unusual formation had been created over millions of years from layers of magma that had oozed to the earth's surface, then cooled, and been subsequently molded by water and wind into the shapes seen today. Rope ladders had been installed in some places to get from one level to the next. The ocean breezes that whistled through the openings felt good on their warm skin. They spent a half hour exploring the nooks and caves and pools before they noticed the first wave of the catamaran crowd snorkeling toward the beach. A Zodiac dinghy had been launched as well from a yacht moored offshore. Julia noticed several passengers aboard, accompanied by coolers and a pile of colorful towels.

"Time to go, Carly. Let's find that other beach and swim with the manta rays."

"Antonio said there's a trail from here, but I'd rather take the scooters around by the road so we don't have to double back."

"Good plan. We'll have a shorter distance to walk lugging our gear both ways."

FIFTEEN MINUTES later they were on the beach in Devil's Bay. The beach of fine, white sand was almost devoid of any other humans. They put on their snorkeling masks and fins and entered the water, which was warm and comforting. "I think I know why they call this area The Baths," said Carly. "The water is almost like bathwater."

Julia chuckled. "I think it's because the locals used to come here and bathe. Maybe pirates did the same thing."

"Of course. Because it's warm like bath-water."

Julia rolled her eyes. "Let's see if the mantas will come and join us."

They paddled further out from the shore and snorkeled lazily in the warm afternoon sun. It wasn't long before several curious mantas came up to them, nudging them, then swimming below them. It was as if they wanted to play tag with the funny-looking humans. When Julia and Carly stood up in waist-deep water, the mantas stayed nearby, frequently swimming close enough to be touched. They seemed to enjoy nuzzling against the girls' legs. Julia noticed that it felt ticklish until she got used to the sensation.

"This is amazing," said Carly. "I'm glad they aren't sharks. I'm not ready to be anybody's dinner."

"Definitely an experience to write up in my journal. But speaking of dinner, I'm hungry. Let's find out what Rita packed in our basket."

The warm sun dried their bodies as they sat cross-legged on the beach towels and dug into the basket from Rita.

"This is yummy," said Carly after her first bite of a shrimp and mango wrap. "I don't know what she used for the dressing, but I want to have one of these again."

"I see spears of pickle and a baggie of homemade cookies when you're ready. And a couple of bottles of pineapple juice. They're still icy cold. Maybe she froze them first."

The sisters devoured the lunch. Something about playing in the water seemed to trigger a bigger appetite than normal. Julia was about to stretch out on her towel when she caught movement from her left. "Don't look now, but we've got company," she said quietly.

"Who?" Carly replied. "Is it someone we know?"

"Julia and Carly!" Noah's voice boomed from the rocks above them. "May I join you?"

"Sure," said Carly. "We were getting lonely on the beach."

Julia glared at her sister. "Not," she whispered gruffly.

Noah was alone. He lugged a duffel bag from which he pulled a towel and a small cooler. Julia couldn't help but notice his toned muscles and chest hair when he pulled off his t-shirt. "I'll share my beer," he said.

"Just what I was wanting. Thank you, Captain Noah." Carly accepted two frosty bottles and handed one of them to Julia.

After toasting each other and the beautiful beach, they swigged the refreshing cold drink.

"Hey, thank you for picking up the tab for our lunch the other day," said Julia.

"Yeah," said Carly. "That was really sweet of you."

"So where's your twin?" asked Julia.

"My twin? I don't have a twin."

"The other captain that we saw on the beach where you were filming looks just like you."

"Oh, my understudy. His name is Luke. He went into town to buy something for his girlfriend back home."

"So you aren't shooting today?" Julia swallowed more of the refreshingly cold local beer.

"There'll be a night shoot sometime later in the evening. The lighting wasn't right when we tried a couple of days ago so Stubby—I mean Brock—wants to try again." Noah chuckled. "We don't call him Stubby to his face, of course, but it suits him."

"We thought the same thing when we first saw him," said Carly. "Is he a good director?"

Noah shrugged. "Probably as good as any in the B movie category."

"Have you done a lot of movies?" asked Julia. "I didn't think to Google your name to find out if you're famous."

Noah laughed. "I keep hoping to land something meatier than what I've done so far. My agent says I've got the right looks and all, but I don't know. It's a hard business to break into if you want to go big time. And I don't have any connections."

"Can you tell us which beach you'll use for the filming tonight?" asked Carly. "I bet I can talk Julia into coming with me. If it's not past her bedtime."

Julia tossed a handful of sand in Carly's direction as she ducked. It totally missed its mark.

"I'm pretty sure it'll be where you found us last time. We have to bury and unbury the same chests over and over until Brock likes how it looks on film." Noah groaned.

"But isn't that done by someone other than the captains?" asked Julia. "Like the swabbies or whatever they're called."

"In pirate days they would be the captives that the ships pick up after taking over another ship. They get to do all the hard work, pretty much. But these guys are actors, not ditch diggers." He smiled with a lop-sided grin. "We all have to pitch in for these scenes."

"Couldn't Brock pay someone else, like a local, to dig most of the hole and then film the part toward the end when the treasure is found by the actors, or vice versa when they're burying it again?"

"In a higher-budget film, yes. With Brock's budget, no." He finished his beer and checked his watch. "I need to get back to catch my ride for the filming later. It takes forever to get makeup and all that done."

"We saw your ship heading that away," said Julia, pointing toward Tortola. "Aren't they going to be in tonight's filming?"

"We're shooting some scenes on Dead Chest Island tomorrow. The sailing crew, the real sailors, are moving the boat to Peter Island for the night. They'll anchor out there so it's not so far to sail the next day."

"How do the rest of you move around?" asked Julia.

"Brock charters boats as he needs them. Tomorrow there'll only be three or four of the pirate crew and Luke and me in one boat. The filming team and makeup and costume people will be on another boat."

"Sounds expensive to have to move all those humans and that gear around."

"Well, Brock wants as much authenticity as possible and Dead Chest Island is where Blackbeard supposedly buried at least some of his loot. Or so legend has it. Anyway, tonight's filming doesn't involve the ship, only a few of us humans. Gotta run." He saluted as he turned to go up the trail.

"If we go tonight, we could ask questions about the costumes they have for women," said Julia to Carly when Noah was out of earshot. "I haven't seen any female characters yet."

"You're right. I wonder what they would be doing in a movie like this."

Julia giggled. "Maybe it's going to have a bodice-ripper scene in it."

Carly scoffed. "The costumes we saw didn't look like bodice-ripper style to me. I thought they looked like what a Chinese concubine might wear. And the shoes looked like they were straight out of an Arabian movie."

Julia shook her head. "I doubt Blackbeard did any shang-haiing in Asia. So why does Brock have those Asian-style dresses for this movie?"

"Beats me, but I wouldn't mind helping Noah with *his* costume," said Carly.

CHAPTER

SIX

J ulia was delighted to find an email from the diocesan office on St. Kitts Island when she and Carly finished their afternoon at the beach. She scanned it quickly and shared the highlights with her sister.

"This is from the librarian. He says that the image on the pendant most likely represents a Portuguese woman, Beloved Princess Joanna, who was revered as a saint even though she was never officially canonized."

"Why would she be called a princess? How does that make any sense?"

"He goes on to say that her father was the king of Portugal so she was royalty. Her older brother died at a very young age so she became heir apparent to the throne, and had the title of princess until a younger brother was born and relieved her of the obligation. Boys first, you know." Julia raised an eyebrow to go with her jaded smile. "Anyway, she lived from 1452 to 1490, which puts her in the fifteenth century. And that's consistent with the time frame Father Lorenzo mentioned."

"And with the Portuguese writing on the back. Did the librarian say what that meant?"

"Yes. 'God be with you always.'"

"Interesting. The question remains as to how our Jane Doe ended up with it."

"It does indeed."

AFTER ANOTHER DELICIOUS meal of grilled sea bass, rice, tropical fruits and mango sorbet, Julia and Carly set off for the beach to watch the filming of the pirate treasure burial. Or un-burial, depending on what was happening by the time they got there.

As they walked through the sand to the film site, Carly asked Julia, "What did Father Lorenzo say when you called him to ask about Saint Princess Joanna?"

"He said she was a strong figure for the young women of the islands who, because of the local culture, were subject to the bidding of their fathers or older brothers."

"Did he mean in the fifteenth century, or now?"

"Both, probably. Look ahead. Noah is coming this way."

Noah smiled broadly as he approached the sisters. "Looks like you got past the guards at the gate."

Julia and Carly looked at each other. Julia replied, "There was a gate?"

"Just kidding. Come on down to the beach. We're about to unbury the treasure we buried yesterday. Again." He rolled his eyes and led them closer to the filming crew. "You can sit in these chairs behind Stubby—uh, Brock. He never sits down anyway so he won't even know you're here."

Julia and Carly smiled at the three men behind the cameras and accepted cold bottles of water as they sat down.

"This is exciting," said Carly. "I can't wait to tell my friends that we got to watch a real movie being filmed. It's a first for me."

"You don't count being filmed when we were onstage for our dances on the cruise ship?"

"We weren't being filmed for a movie."

"Sure we were. They ran those videos night and day."

"And destroyed them when they hit port and started over. Not the same thing, sister."

Julia accepted defeat and turned to watch the pirates take their positions, shovels in hand, waiting for Brock's cue to start action. She assumed they were digging a hole for the treasure chest which sat on the sand a couple of feet away.

"Scene seventeen, take three. Action!" Brock barked out the command and retreated about twenty feet away from the actors.

Three scruffy pirates took turns scooping shovelfuls of sand. They moved rhythmically in the gentle breeze, grunting regularly. Julia started humming "Fifteen Men on a Dead Man's Chest" but a glare from Carly ended her serenade.

A couple of minutes later they heard a metallic clank and a shriek as one of the pirates jerked backward, dropped his shovel, and fell to the sand. Brock yelled, "Cut," and hurried to where the hole was being dug. He gasped and gestured for his assistant director to join him.

Everyone on the set moved in to see what was going on, including Julia and Carly. Luke knelt down and scooped enough sand away from whatever the shovel had struck to reveal the object. Then he sat back with a frown. All eyes were on a treasure chest sitting deep in the sand with a half-buried silver slipper next to it. Carly looked at Julia, who just shrugged.

"What's wrong, Mr. Hughes?" asked Julia.

Brock mopped his brow with an oversized handkerchief.

"It's not one of our treasure chests. Someone else must have buried it."

Noah stood with his hands on his hips, legs akimbo. "Perhaps we should call the police and let them handle this. I don't want to have my fingerprints on it if there's real booty inside."

"Someone's playing a practical joke on us," scoffed Luke.

Brock gave him an icy stare. "I certainly hope not. We're already behind schedule and over budget. This is not a time for jokes." He stormed away, punching numbers on the cell phone in his hand.

Julia and Carly moved closer to Noah and caught his attention. He joined them where they were standing, about fifteen feet away from the treasure chest. "What is it?" he asked.

"That's the same kind of slipper that was at the other beach where we found the dead young lady," said Julia.

"No jumping to conclusions," warned Carly.

"I'm just making an observation. I wonder what's in the chest. I wish we could open it and peek."

"Me too," said Noah, "but I'm sure Brock is calling the police already. All we can do is wait."

FIFTEEN MINUTES later police sirens blared through the otherwise silent air. Drew, the police chief, and another officer named Ray joined the small crowd and got a brief history from Brock. After taking several photos of the scene, Drew picked up the single shoe and handed it to Ray to bag as evidence.

He directed the pirate crew to continue digging around the chest until it could be lifted from its sandy grave.

Julia guessed it was quite heavy from the grunts of the two men assigned to move the chest to the surface. Drew nodded to Lenny, who removed the metal bar from the primitive closure and slowly lifted the domed lid of the black chest. Drew and Lenny gasped at the same moment. Drew's face paled as he closed the lid again.

"What did you find?" asked Brock. "Was there anything in it?"

"Drugs in packets. Tablets that look like prescription meds." Drew nodded to Julia. "Like we talked about earlier. We'll have to test them but it's probably cocaine or fentanyl. Or both. That's what we're finding in most of our drug busts these days." He shook his head. "And some jewelry that looks quite old. But it probably isn't." Drew scratched his forehead and put his hat back on his head. "We'll take possession of the chest and store it until we can get testing done and have the jewelry analyzed."

"What about the slipper?" asked Julia. "It's just like the other one from Savannah Beach."

"Yes, I noticed. It may well be the mate to the one we have at the station. I'll check it out when we get there."

As the police officers took their leave with the chest in the back of their SUV, Brock gathered the actors and cameramen around him.

"I don't feel much like continuing tonight," he said. "I think we got good enough footage of the digging for now and can shoot more film later if needed. Get some rest tonight so we can catch up to our schedule tomorrow on Dead Chest Island."

Noah hung back from the rest of the actors as they walked to their vehicles. "Hey, Julia and Carly. Are you in a hurry?"

"No," said Julia. "Why?"

"Meet me at the Sapphire in about twenty minutes. I have something to tell you."

CHAPTER
SEVEN

J ulia's antennae quivered as she and Carly rode the
scooters back to The Sapphire Lighthouse Bar in Spanish
Town. Noah had arrived before them and sat at a table
with three frosty draft beers waiting.

He stood and greeted each of them with a hug and peck on
the cheek. His face clouded a little as he raised his glass in a
half-hearted toast to his friends.

"You look worried," said Julia. "Or maybe it's sadness that I
see."

Noah smiled thinly. "Both. I didn't want to admit that I had
maybe seen the girl that you found on the beach. But when
that shoe showed up today, I felt bad that I had lied."

"I'm listening," said Julia.

"Well, I don't actually know that it was *her*, but I had seen
a girl hanging around the film crew a couple of times earlier
last week. She could have taken shoes from the costume tent
when no one was there. You've been there and could see how
easy it would have been for someone to wander in and out
without anybody noticing."

"Do you know anything about her? Was she friendly with someone?"

"That's all I know. And it might not be the girl you found, but the shoe ... it looks like one of ours." Noah looked at Julia, then down at his feet. He wore slip-on Sperry boat shoes without socks.

"That reminds me," said Julia. "Why are there costumes for women? I haven't seen any females around except in the makeup tent."

Noah snorted. "Brock has this crazy idea about putting Chinese concubines in the script. I don't think he gets that the shanghaied stories wouldn't have happened here. China's a long way away! The pirates here were more the buccaneer, plundering type. Anyway, he's talked about hiring some local girls for a couple of scenes. But he's had trouble finding Asians here." He shook his head. "As I said before, he's a B movie director. Doesn't plan ahead."

"So, the young woman is probably a local girl."

"I guess."

"Have you seen any other girls or women hanging around while you've been filming?"

"Oh, yeah." Noah rolled his head all the way around and took a long swig of his beer. "Not the last few days, but when we were shooting some footage on the other side of the island last week, quite a few young people were nosing around. They looked like teenagers to me, looking for some action. The security guard kept chasing them off, but they'd sneak back and stay just out of sight of Brock and the guard."

Julia felt her antennae quiver harder. "Did you notice anything in particular about the girl you saw?" She showed him the photo in which the young woman looked like she was sleeping, rather than dead.

Noah shuddered and looked away quickly after he glanced

at the picture. "I didn't pay much attention to individual people. Maybe the security guard would recognize her face and remember more than I do."

"That's a good idea," said Julia. "I'll suggest that to Drew."

"There were definitely more guys hanging around than girls, but I haven't seen any of them recently, like I said. They seem to have disappeared this week." He checked his watch and stood. "Gotta run. Early start tomorrow on Dead Chest Island."

He slurped down the rest of his beer and nodded as he strode out of the bar. "See ya around."

Once he was out of hearing range, Julia said, "He seems more nervous than I think he would be if he truly didn't have any more contact with our Jane Doe than he says." She sat back with the beer which had long since lost its froth. She signaled to the waitress for a fresh cold one.

Carly nodded. "I think so, too. But why would he even bother to tell us anything?"

"I wonder if he knows more and is covering up for someone, but wants to get something off his chest."

"Yeah. It's not like he gave us any useful information."

"Back to square one, I guess," said Julia. "This beer is so much better when it's icy cold like this one."

"Maybe Drew will have had some luck with identifying the girl. It's been a couple of days since he circulated her picture."

"True. We need to tell him what we found out about the pendant anyway."

～

TUESDAY

At breakfast the next morning Antonio told the sisters that he had a surprise lined up for them. Julia and Carly

55

looked at each other with excited grins. They both loved surprises.

"One of my friends owns a sweet restaurant called Sidney's Peace and Love on Jost Van Dyke. It's another island that's easily reachable by boat. I would love to take you there for lunch if you don't have anything else planned today."

"Other than a quick visit with the police chief, we're free." Julia turned to Carly. "Right?"

Carly was grinning and bobbing her golden curls.

"It's a good hour or so with our powerboat unless the current and the wind are both against us, but I've checked the weather forecast and today is the best of the next several days, weather-wise." He searched the girls' eyes.

Julia and Carly looked at each other again and nodded eagerly. "Mom always said to jump at this kind of opportunity because it might not happen again."

"Bellissimo! We need to leave here at about ten a.m. I'll call the marina and have them get my boat ready. You can meet me there."

Julia raised her eyebrows at that. She wondered what kind of boat he had that earned him such personal attention. Or maybe that was commonplace here.

"Carly, let's scoot into town and see if we can catch Drew at the police station before we go to the marina."

Drew was on a phone call when they arrived. He turned to them and indicated they could sit down and wait a couple of minutes. He stood at his desk and gazed out the window as he talked, nodding from time to time. From the conversation, Julia was able to discern that he was talking with someone from Tortola.

He sat down and leaned back in his chair when he ended the call. "That was the police chief in Road Town. He has a lead on the identity of the girl but needs to follow up with another bit of information before he's ready to approach her parents."

"That's got to be a hard part of your job, informing parents."

Drew nodded soberly. "That it is. So what's on your mind today?"

Julia told him about the icon and inscription on the pendant found near the girl. "It seems fairly certain that the necklace is probably old and valuable. I'm hoping to learn something from a shop in San Juan that specializes in vintage and antique jewelry."

"If it *is* old pirate treasure, I'd like to know where she got it. Especially since the treasure chest that was dug up last night had some jewelry in it, as well as the drugs." Drew sat forward, leaning on his elbows, and smiled. "Maybe we'll get lucky and trace something down."

"Maybe it's all connected," said Julia. "Whoever buried that chest is hopping mad, I'm sure, to have you take possession of that loot. The street value of the drugs has to be ... what?"

"Tens of thousands of dollars." The Chief filled in the blank.

Carly added, "Plus, I bet it'll be hard to keep it secret, with the film crew and actors having been there when you took it."

Drew snorted. "It's under lock and key for now, but at some point we'll have to deal with disposing of it. The jewelry will go to the central office in Road Town, and they'll get it appraised. Please let me know what you find out, will ya? I can use the extra eyes and ears." He rose and escorted them out.

～

ANTONIO'S POWERBOAT turned out to be a forty-foot luxury yacht christened *Wind Spirit* with a cruising speed of thirty knots. The azure blue of the Caribbean whizzed by as Julia and Carly sipped on the tropical drinks thoughtfully provided by Rita. The breeze ruffled their hair and kept them comfortable in the otherwise eighty-degree heat. Antonio pointed out the other islands as they sped through the water. Scrub Island and Great Camanoe Island were on their right, with Beef Island—at the east end of Tortola—on the left. Soon they were abreast of the main part of Tortola on their left, with Guana Island on the right. He pointed out some of the main beaches and features of Tortola.

"This is wonderful, Antonio," said Julia. "I was expecting a much smaller boat like some of my friends have on the Columbia River. Not a luxury yacht."

"Thank you, my friend. A larger boat is more practical here. When we use it for transportation between islands it's really much safer, especially in rougher seas, and we can travel faster as well."

"It's quite a treat for us," said Julia.

"It's my pleasure, ladies." He smiled and tipped his captain's hat as they continued to move through the water. "Today you'll enjoy a lovely lobster lunch at Sidney's Peace and Love. Rita and I go there once a month just to remind ourselves of the freedom we have here. To go from island to island where cars cannot go. Even small airplanes can't always go to places like this. There's no place to land."

"A seaplane, maybe?"

Antonio arched an eyebrow. "A boat is much easier and more practical, in my opinion. Our destination is just ahead. Grab those binoculars and look in the direction where you see the small flotilla of boats. That's where we're going."

Julia scanned the horizon and found the restaurant's sign

above the small group of boats of all sizes. She pulled the binoculars from her eyes for a moment and looked off to the west.

"What is it?" asked Carly. "You look puzzled."

Julia looked through the binoculars again, then handed them to her sister. "Look between the islands, about one-third of the way from the island to the right. Isn't that our pirate ship?"

EIGHT

Carly surveyed the horizon to the west of their location and nodded when she spotted the ship. "Sure looks like it. Although there could be other pirate ships just like it in other ports. Like replicas of the *Lady Washington* or other square-riggers that we've seen in more than one place."

"True," said Julia, looking through the binoculars once again. "I've seen them in other ports where people can take a ride or have dinner onboard. But it sure looks like the one from the movie."

"Maybe Antonio knows something." Carly turned to where Antonio was driving the boat from the upper captain's seat. "We see a pirate ship farther ahead. It looks like the one that we saw where they're shooting the movie. Is there more than one of them around?"

Antonio picked up his binocs and looked where Carly was pointing. "That's not the one I usually see around here," he said as he focused on his steering. "There's a mostly black ship that sails out of Road Town. It does one-hour sails during the afternoon and a dinner cruise a couple of nights a week, but it's not usually this far out on a weekday. The movie crew boat probably comes out of Puerto Rico. I've heard one or two of them get leased out for that kind of thing. It's probably one of those."

"Thanks. How much longer to get to Sidney's restaurant?"

Antonio smiled as if he'd heard that question many times before. "About ten more minutes. Get your appetite ready."

Carly scrambled back down the ladder to the main cockpit where Julia kept her eye on the pirate boat. Carly related what she'd learned. "Didn't Noah say they would be filming on Dead Chest Island today? Is that nearby?"

Julia pointed to the nautical chart of the British Virgin Islands on the small table. "Dead Chest Island is on the southern side of Tortola, near Peter Island." She stabbed her finger on the map. "That's nowhere close to here. So what's that ship doing up here?" She looked at Carly, who shrugged with her hands in the air.

"Do we care?"

"I suppose not. Maybe Brock had a change in plans. Or maybe they didn't need the ship for today's filming after all."

"We can ask Noah later," said Carly with a flirtatious giggle.

A couple of dockhands showed up as Antonio eased the yacht along the small pier in front of Sidney's. Julia had helped moor boats in the past and eagerly helped the young men secure the *Wind Spirit*. She announced that she could tie a bowline knot, but Antonio said it wasn't needed today.

Julia and Carly followed their host up the ramp to the busy restaurant. A maitre d' greeted them with, "Antonio! Welcome!

And where is your lovely wife today?" He showed them to a table with a magnificent view of the water.

"Rita is busy today with her garden club and said I could come with my new friends if I promised to behave." He winked at the girls. "This is Julia on my right, and her sister Carly—the blonde one. Ladies, meet Eduardo."

"Pleased to meet you, Eduardo," said Julia. "This is lovely."

"Where's Sidney?" asked Carly, looking around.

Eduardo laughed. "Who needs Sidney? You've got me!"

Antonio explained that Sidney often didn't come in until it was time for the evening crowd. "But the lobster will be just as delicious, I assure you."

Eduardo took drink orders, offering a draft beer and several special cocktails. They all opted for the lobster as recommended by Antonio—it was the house specialty, after all.

"You said that you and Rita come over here regularly," said Julia. "Is it because of the lobster or do you have another reason?"

"Yes, because of the food and also because Rita gets tired of cooking day after day. In addition to that, we have limited choices for dine-out on our island."

Carly raised her hand. "I can identify with that! We only have three restaurants and a couple of fast-food options in my little town. It's a nuisance to drive farther away, especially when we're hungry."

"I second that," said Julia. "I'm too tired to enjoy cooking after a long day at the clinic, and it isn't fun to go out by myself, now that I'm not dating anyone. But I really enjoy getting to go to a grand restaurant now and then. With good company, especially."

"Miss Julia," said Antonio, "I cannot believe there isn't a line of young men wanting to fall in love with you."

Julia blushed. "There's a very small pool of eligible men in

Parkview, and most of them would be intimidated around me, I'm afraid. And the ones who aren't are either eighty years old or married or otherwise unsuitable. Trust me when I say I'm not in a hurry." She waved her hand as if brushing off a fly.

Eduardo arrived with a tray of colorful drinks. "Here's Antonio's beer and a few samples of several specialty cocktails. Tell me if you like them. My bartender is always making up new concoctions."

Julia selected a pretty, blue drink and Carly opted for a raspberry-colored blend in a stemmed glass. Antonio picked up his beer.

"Cheers to a lovely, sunny day in this beautiful part of the world," said Julia.

"With my friends," added Antonio.

Julia and Carly tasted each other's drink, then each took one of the other two selections, again sharing tastes. Antonio sat back and smiled, enjoying watching the sisters taste the Caribbean cocktails. When Eduardo returned to see how they liked the flavors, Carly ordered a Painkiller and Julia opted for an Aruba Arriba.

"It's a good thing I'm not driving back," said Julia. "I might flunk a sobriety test if I were stopped."

"I would intervene for you, my friend, but that never happens around here," said Antonio.

"Why not? I can imagine a lot of alcohol being consumed on the charter boats around here."

"Yes, but most of them are smart enough to stay in harbor or on anchor when they've been drinking. Too many areas with shallow reefs and sunken boats to risk moving on the water, especially after sunset."

"What about the locals?" asked Carly. "Do they follow the same rules?"

"The smart ones, yes, or if they want to live to a ripe old age, like me." Antonio chuckled.

Julia protested. "You must be all of fifty."

Antonio cocked his head. "That's kind of you. Ah, here comes our food."

Julia and Carly stared at the huge platter of lobster that was placed in front of them. There were individual bowls of melted butter—the best part of eating lobster in Julia's opinion—in addition to side dishes of risotto and fresh local vegetables. Eduardo added a basket of warm bread fresh from the oven.

Antonio chuckled at the look of sheer joy on the faces of his guests as he raised his glass and said, "Let's eat."

TWENTY MINUTES LATER, with sticky fingers and butter dripping off their chins, the three of them ate the last of the succulent meal. Julia groaned when Eduardo suggested dessert. "I'll explode. I swear."

Carly added, "Thanks anyway. That was amazingly good."

Antonio took care of the bill while Julia and Carly walked along the dock. The pirate ship was nowhere in sight.

Once they had cast off and were on their way out of the harbor, Antonio asked, "Would you like to go a little farther along the island and check out our local legend, Foxy? He has a bar around the next bend in Great Harbor. Maybe we'll get lucky and you'll see that pirate ship again."

"Do we have to eat?" Carly held her hand palm-down at the level of her throat, reminding him that she was stuffed.

"We don't even have to stop. We can cruise along the coast and look at the scenery."

"Sounds good," said Julia.

"Although he might know something about the pirate ship," said Antonio. "Just a thought." He deftly steered the yacht along the western entrance to Garner Bay, picking up speed as he moved into the open water, then headed west along the southern side of Jost Van Dyke Island.

A short fifteen minutes later, Antonio turned *Wind Spirit* into Great Harbor. Julia and Carly admired the tropical setting with houses nestled amongst the palms on the banks. Dozens of sailboats and powerboats bobbed in the harbor where they were anchored out.

"It would be heavenly to wake up here in the morning with the blue sky and nothing more complicated to do than put on a bathing suit and lie in the sun," said Julia.

"You're forgetting about cooking."

"I'll have a boat big enough for a maid."

"What about seasonal hurricanes?"

"I'll move my boat."

"What about provisions when you run out of food?"

"I'll order from Amazon."

"And how will they deliver it to you?"

"Okay, Carly. This is *my* fantasy, so Amazon can deliver anywhere."

"Sheesh. And you're supposed to be the practical one."

Antonio slowed the motor to the requisite five MPH as they neared a dock with a big sign that read Foxy's. Right behind it stood a rustic building that looked like it might blow down in the next big storm.

"Let's tie up for a few minutes," said Antonio. "I need to talk to Foxy, myself."

The threesome trekked the short distance to the beach shack. The dilapidated building was huge on the inside compared to its deceptive exterior size. The decor was a mix of yacht club burgees, license plates and a mix of decals. There were captain's hats, baseball hats, bikini bottoms and tank tops hanging from the rafters.

The daytime crowd was eclectic, to say the least: clusters of young guys laughing and drinking beer, sitting next to older and middle-aged men talking loudly, also drinking beer. Julia saw several couples sitting at a high-top table enjoying beer (the men) and pretty cocktails (the ladies). She wondered if they had come in by dinghy from one of the big sailboats in the harbor. Antonio led them to the bar in the back, where a man of indeterminate age leaned against the polished wood.

"Julia and Carly, meet Foxy. He's the proprietor of this lovely business."

Foxy was gray-haired, with a big smile peeking from his beard. "Welcome. A friend of Antonio's is a friend of mine. Let me offer you a beer." He turned to a bartender on his left. "Miguel. Bring cold beers for my guests and me. Cooper Island."

Foxy led his guests to a table not far from a door marked "Private." Miguel arrived with four mugs of the local beer almost before they sat down.

"These lovely ladies want to know more about the pirate ships from Puerto Rico," said Antonio after a proper toast. "I thought you might know something."

"Oh, yes. I heard they are making a movie and doing some filming on Virgin Gorda and maybe on Tortola also." Foxy pulled his spectacles from a pocket and peered closely at Julia and Carly. "Are you two beauties wanting to be movie stars? I have a friend in the business."

"He has a friend in every business," Antonio interjected.

Foxy threw his shoulders back and laughed loudly.

Julia jumped at the sudden sound and sloshed her beer. "No, nothing like that. We met some of the crew and actors on

Virgin Gorda and saw their ship sailing this way earlier today. Did you see it?"

"Not today, but I wasn't watching for it. It comes and goes. Sometimes one way, sometimes another. But I don't know anything more." Foxy turned and asked Miguel, who hovered behind him. "What about you?"

"No, nothing more than you," said Miguel.

Foxy had a quizzical look on his sun-bronzed face. Then he looked at the sisters and with a smile began to point towards some of the items displayed on the walls. Soon he was regaling the women with stories, both humorous and a few slightly lewd, of how each came to decorate his bar.

Finally, Antonio downed his beer and said, "Well, time to head back home before the water gets too rough with the late-afternoon winds. Are you ready, ladies?"

Julia and Carly nodded. "Thanks, Foxy. Nice to meet you," said Julia.

"My little ladybirds," said Antonio, "I need a word with Foxy before we leave. I'll catch up with you in a few minutes."

The sisters strolled down the sandy trail toward the pier.

Julia asked, "Did you see the look on Foxy's face when Miguel made a comment about the pirate ship?"

"Yeah. It's like Miguel knows something."

Antonio rejoined them as they continued walking back to the yacht. "The weather report has changed from earlier in the day. The winds are picking up from the east. I don't think we will see rain but there could be a squall between here and Spanish Town. I'll keep an eye on those dark clouds south of us. Let's hurry."

CHAPTER
NINE

J ulia and Carly manned the lines and cast off from the small dock. They could feel the change in the marine air from a mere thirty minutes earlier. It was a few degrees cooler and the wind had shifted directions, now coming from the southeast.

Antonio guided the yacht along the shore's edge for a short distance before turning back toward Virgin Gorda.

Julia pointed to a small establishment on the beach. "Tipsy Shark," she read the name aloud. "What does that remind you of, Carly?"

"What a coincidence. I think we were meant to see that name after our adventure with Kate last year."

"What adventure are you talking about?" asked Antonio. "Who's Kate?"

Julia gave him a thumbnail sketch of their trip to Paris, Roger's death, and Kate's parents' business in Cape Cod called The Drunken Shark.

"I wonder how Kate is doing," said Carly.

"Better than Pierre, I'd bet," said Julia. "He's probably still wearing orange."

"Or whatever color bad guys wear in French jails."

Antonio shook his head. "And now you have found another dead body. Is it possible that you have bad karma, Miss Julia?"

THE RETURN TRIP to Spanish Town was uneventful despite the rougher water and heavier winds. The dockhands at the marina took care of *Wind Spirit* while Antonio and his house-guests went on to the bed-and-breakfast.

"I expect you are tired after a day on the water and might want to rest. I am busy away from the house the rest of the day so please make yourself at home." Antonio set out a plate of snacks that Rita had prepared. "Rita is with her sister and will be home later this evening. She thought you might want something light to eat after our lobster lunch. And of course, there's beer and a pitcher of Mojitos in the fridge." He gave a polite salute and left Julia and Carly in the kitchen.

"I'm not hungry yet but I want to try a Mojito," said Carly. "I bet they taste better here than at home."

"It's only three thirty. Do you want to find a beach and work on our suntans?"

"We could check out that beach we were heading for the day we found Jane Doe. Antonio said besides being off the beaten path, it has a small coral reef to explore. Maybe we'll see something interesting."

"I'll grab the sunscreen. And we can take the Mojitos in insulated cups. I saw some in the pantry."

THE WALK to the beach along Savannah Bay seemed shorter this time now that they knew their way around better. Julia and Carly slowed down when they neared the rock where they'd found the body. There wasn't a trace of her previous presence. They picked up the pace after a cursory look at the site. Julia felt a shiver go down her spine despite the warm temperature. She sensed a sinister aura lingering in the immediate area.

The aquamarine water of the Caribbean sparkled in the late afternoon sun. The gray clouds had dissipated, leaving fat, puffy, marshmallow clouds in their place. A gentle breeze fluttered across the sand. The white-sand beach was nearly deserted on the southern end. A few people with beach chairs and umbrellas lounged lazily several hundred yards away near the opposite end.

Julia and Carly, slathered with SPF 50 sunscreen, stretched out on their striped beach towels, Mojitos in hand. A few birds chattered at each other; otherwise, a peaceful silence surrounded them.

The roar of a powerboat screamed through the air. Julia opened an evil eye at the offending sound, then sat up and shook Carly. "Isn't that Antonio's boat?" She pointed to the noisemaker which was moving from left to right.

"Looks too small to me, but I can't read the name from this far away. There are probably a lot of boats just like it around here."

"You're probably right." Julia settled into a comfortable position in the soft sand. "You know, that seems like an expensive boat for someone who runs a bed-and-breakfast inn. I wonder if he made a lot of money at another job before this."

"You think too much. Maybe his wife is the one with the money."

"Yeah. Maybe that's it. They seem really young to have made tons of money and be retired already, though."

"Do you have a point, Julia, or are you just nosy?"

"I wonder how long they've lived here and where they came from."

"Julia ..."

"All right, I'll shut up."

A few perfectly peaceful moments passed before the tune of a mournful harmonica disturbed the quiet solitude.

"Stop playing that thing," said a deep male voice. "You're in enough trouble already without hurting my ears."

"It wasn't my fault they found the trunk," a second voice whined.

"You buried it on the wrong beach, numb-nuts," said Deep Voice. "The *fake* chests were supposed to be buried where they did the filming last night. Not the real ones."

Julia and Carly looked at each other with big eyes. They were lying behind a small dune on the beach and didn't think they were visible—at least, not yet—to the approaching voices.

"Do we have to dithappear?" lisped a third voice.

"No one's going to disappear," said the second voice, "as long as we follow directions."

"Boss said to check out Mountain Trunk Bay," said Deep Voice. "He wants to be sure we can make the transfer there. This beach looks too busy."

"Yeth, he did. We better do what we're thuppothed to do."

Deep Voice said, "Yeah, yeah, yeah. You two are just wimps." He exhaled loudly. "Okay. We've got a couple of hours to get it done."

Julia and Carly held perfectly still for several more minutes before daring to sit up cautiously and survey the beach for the three men. They saw no one, but being extra cautious, they stayed put for another ten minutes. They didn't want to chance running into them at the beach trailhead, even though Julia wanted to see what they looked like.

"You'll have to be content with knowing their voices instead of their faces," said Carly. "I still want to snorkel. I know you likely want to talk to Drew again, but really, there's little we can tell him from that snatch of conversation anyway. We can tell him later, right?"

"Yes, I agree. But the water looks snarly out there. It might be a reaction to the wind earlier. Maybe tomorrow."

"Really?" Carly groused. "Our vacation is almost over. It's halfway through the week and we haven't snorkeled enough to bother to count."

"Yes, but look at that suntan you're getting." Julia motioned to her sister's body as if showcasing it and got a grin and a pose from Carly.

The two of them retraced their steps to where they'd parked their scooters. As they neared the rock where they'd found the dead girl, Julia paused and sniffed the air. "Do you notice anything in the air, Carly? It smells like something burning right here."

Carly obligingly inhaled a lungful of air and promptly started coughing. "Yes. I think it's an herb of some kind." She looked around at the ground. "I don't *see* anything burning. There's no smoke."

Julia noticed some movement out of the corner of her eye. She looked to the left and saw a figure moving stealthily through the heavy brush and trees and away from the rock.

"Hello! We won't hurt you. Can we talk?"

The stooped woman's figure stopped moving and slowly turned around. She stared at Julia and Carly. After a moment she took a big breath and walked slowly back toward the rock. She wore a dark toga-like garment with a scarf over her head. She held something smoking in her hand.

Julia and Carly stood still and waited for the dark-skinned woman to enter the clearing. The wrinkled face of an older person was framed by wisps of graying hair peeking out from the front of the scarf. She wore scuffed moccasins.

The woman stopped at the end of the huge rock. She remained silent.

"Did you know the young lady who was on the rock?" Julia asked quietly. "Do you speak English?"

The woman cocked her head. "Are you friends of the young lady?" Her English had the lilt of the local dialect. It fell gently on Julia's ears.

"I'm sorry that we didn't know her, but we found her here on the rock. We went to the police and told them. Did you know her?"

The woman shook her head, her face flat. "No, she is from another island, but she is one of the descendants of the Arawak tribe who lived here before the white man came."

"Do you know her name? We're helping the police try to identify her so they can notify her family. They must be worried."

"I don't know *her* name, but her family lives on Tortola. They are Lejeune."

"Thank you. Who are you? My name is Julia and this is my sister Carly." Carly smiled and nodded as she was introduced. "Are you Arawak?"

The woman stood a little straighter. "I am Amaya, descended from the Great Shaman of my tribe. His spirit lives in me. He sent me here to remove the bad spirits."

"What are you burning?" asked Carly. "It smells like an herb but I can't identify it."

The spirit woman held up the bunch of smoking branches. "It is sage. The smoke sends the bad spirits away so this place can feel peaceful again."

"I like that idea," said Julia. "Can we help you?"

Amaya handed each girl a couple of twigs with smoking leaves. "Do the same as I do. Wave the smoke in front of you and walk slowly around the rock. This was an altar of sacrifice in the days of the Arawak. The sage will cleanse the air so my ancestors can rest again. We will walk three times around the rock."

Julia and Carly solemnly followed Amaya as she circled the rock. She chanted as she raised and lowered her arms, sending the smoke in arcs through the air, three revolutions in all. When she stopped at the edge of the clearing where she'd started, she held out her hands and gestured that they should give her the rest of the smoking herb. She flicked the burning ends against the rock, rubbed the ends to remove any embers, then opened a small leather pouch into which she put the remnants of the sage and pulled it closed.

Amaya bowed slightly and turned to go back into the brush from whence she had come. Just before she melted into the tropical foliage, she stopped and said, "May you learn the truth."

The sisters stood silent for a moment, entranced.

"That was amazing," said Carly. "I've got goosebumps."

"And we've got a name for Drew, or at least a last name. Let's get back to town. We can tell him about those other guys, too."

"Yeah. He can follow up on it. I don't want to take a chance on running into them on a lonely beach."

CHAPTER
TEN

Antonio and Rita were both still gone when Julia and Carly traipsed in from the beach. The sisters cleaned up and changed into street clothes for a trip into town to grab a quick meal before stopping by the police station.

The sun was sinking lower in the sky by the time they pulled into the Sapphire, where they promptly ran into the police chief. He invited them to join him at his table.

"Just the man we wanted to talk with," said Julia after ordering two Mojitos from the waitress. "We overheard some men talking at the beach on Savannah Bay this afternoon."

"We didn't see their faces, though, " added Carly.

"I'm not understanding what this is about," said Drew, shaking his head.

Julia took a big breath and added the details from the conversation they'd overheard. "It sure sounded like it's related to the treasure chest that the movie crew dug up last evening."

Drew nodded, a grim smile on his face. "I'd certainly like to know who that drug stash belongs to. Did you hear any names?"

"No," said Julia. "One of them referred to someone they called 'boss' but we didn't hear any other details. They didn't call each other by name, but one of them had a serious lisp. I'd recognize that voice again, I think."

"One of them played a harmonica. Rather badly," said Carly.

"Well, that's not much to go on, but I appreciate the information." He pulled a draw of the beer that had accompanied his meal of fish and chips.

"Oh, and we ran into a spirit woman, like a medicine woman, and she told us that the dead girl was a member of the Lejeune family on Tortola," said Julia.

"Tell me more."

"She didn't know the first name. She was burning sage around that rock where we found her to cleanse it of bad spirits."

Drew scoffed. "Do you believe that kind of stuff?"

Julia smiled and raised an eyebrow. "I've heard stranger things. I have a neighbor at home who swore that ghosts of the previous owners were hanging around her house. Her dog kept growling and snarling at something in the corner of her bedroom. One of her friends told her it might be a ghost, of the previous owner perhaps, and to go to a local store to buy some sage. She said they told her that the smoke of the burning sage will chase ghosts away."

"And?"

"She did that and afterwards Hayley, her dog, stopped growling at the corner. But then she started acting weird in the backyard, as if the ghosts had set up shop there. Ruth burned more sage in the backyard, especially in the corner that the dog was avoiding. Afterwards she said Hayley sniffed the air and sat down and wagged her tail. She's been a normal dog ever since."

"Really?"

"Just reporting what she said," said Julia with a shrug. "Is that any stranger than how acupuncture works? That's mysterious to me."

Drew finished his beer and the rest of his French fries. "I'll chat with the chief in Road Town and ask about the Lejeune family. Maybe that's the name of one of his missing girls. I'll keep you posted," he said as he stood.

"Sure thing," said Julia. Drew left, passing the waitress who was heading to the table with their drinks and to take their food order.

"I don't understand how Drew can be so laid back in investigating the dead girl, and now the whole treasure chest thing." Julia sat with her chin resting on her hand, elbow on the table. "What else does he have to do?"

"You don't know what the rest of his day is like. He could be really busy for all we know."

"But there's a young woman who died unnecessarily due to drugs, a treasure chest full of drugs, and no obvious leads to tie them together. He said, *maybe* that's the name of one of the missing girls, but, gosh, I'd think he'd be familiar enough with those names already to recognize it if it fit."

"Didn't you tell me that when you were in St. Maarten, you were told that there's a lot of drug trafficking going on in the Caribbean and that the authorities can't stop all of it?"

"Yes, because the drug traffickers use planes and yachts and locals to move their product from place to place. They hide behind legitimate business fronts and carry on pretty much unrestricted."

"Well," said Carly, "I can see how that would be pretty hard to control. Fast boats and seaplanes can go a lot of places here in the islands without being detected."

The waitress returned with a plate of nachos with shrimp, avocado, and cheese.

"A perfect meal to end the day," said Carly, looking over her sister's shoulder as she took the first bite. "Don't look now, sis, but we're about to have company. Again."

Julia feigned surprise when Noah grabbed the chair vacated by Drew and invited himself to the table. He'd already gotten a beer from the bartender and took a long swallow as he settled into the chair.

"Hi," said Carly. "How did the filming go on Dead Chest Island today?"

"It was pretty lame. No dead bodies and no beatings of prisoners." He smirked. "And no surprises with the treasure chest this time. Brock was happy about that. He's trying to make up for time that we lost last week when the weather was lousy, and was worried because the forecast for today looked marginal."

"We saw a pirate ship near Jost Van Dyke earlier today," said Julia. "Was that yours?"

"I don't know, actually. We didn't use the ship today, after all. Brock mentioned something about only doing beach shots because the ship's crew had another job."

"Antonio told us that there are other pirate ships that sail back and forth from San Juan so it could have been one of those," said Carly.

"What were you doing at Jost Van Dyke? Did you visit Foxy's?" He smiled and wiggled an eyebrow. "I've heard there's a lot of action there."

"We're not into action, whatever that is," said Julia with narrowed eyes. "Antonio treated us to a lobster feast at

Sidney's, then he took us to Foxy's because he said he needed to talk with him."

"We had a beer there, if that's what you mean by action," said Carly. She slid the plate of nachos toward Noah.

Noah laughed. "Not exactly, Carly. I've heard some of the locals talk about obtaining drugs through connections there even though they're illegal around here."

Julia scoffed. "In my business, I've had to come to grips with the fact that making drugs illegal doesn't make them unobtainable. People who want them manage to find dealers who are willing to take their money and fade back into the woodwork."

"That was an expensive pile of drugs in the chest we dug up last night," said Noah. "I'm sure someone is hopping mad about how that got bungled up."

"Yes, but sadly, I'll bet the dealer knows where to get more," said Julia. "The supply chain never seems to stop."

Carly licked some sauce from her fingers. "Yum. Where are you filming tomorrow?"

"Brock wants to go back to the first place you found us. He's got something cooked up with some dancers from a local studio."

"Will they be dancing?" asked Carly.

"I don't think so. But it's the best he could come up with to line up some females to act as concubines." He finished his beer. "Maybe I'll see you tomorrow. I get to be in full swashbuckling regalia, I'm told." He winked at Carly. "See ya."

"A dance studio, huh?" said Julia after Noah left. "Maybe we can talk our way into the movie. We know a thing or two about dancing."

"Dancing got us into trouble in Germany. Remember?"

"But it was a lot of fun!" Julia grinned at her sister, who

had been kidnapped and held prisoner on that trip. Then she said soberly, "Well, maybe not all of it was fun."

"We'll just watch. After we do some snorkeling. Time is running out and I don't have my quota of suntan yet."

Julia checked email when they got back to the house with its wi-fi connection. "Here's a note from one of the antiquities shops in San Juan. They've attached a photo of a necklace that looks similar to the one we found with the girl." She enlarged the photo attachment and showed it to her sister.

"Yes, it *does* look a lot like it." Carly frowned. "Doesn't it seem unusual that there would be two pendants so similar? It's not like they had commercial jewelry stores in those days."

"That's true, but the jewelers of the day had developed casting by the fifteenth century. They would have been able to make multiple pendants, for example, of one design. They would start with the basic shape and adorn it with jewels, depending on what the customer wanted. Each one would still be unique, but perhaps similar to others made by the same craftsman."

"I'm guessing that the commoners of the time didn't wear much jewelry," said Carly. "It had to be expensive."

"Right you are. The cost would limit its ownership to nobility and the wealthy of the time. Talking about expensive, the dealer says he would be happy to give us more information if we're interested in purchasing this elegant piece." Julia laughed and said, "I don't think so." She pulled up the photo of the necklace they found on the beach for comparison. "The saints look very much alike."

"Saint Ursula, wasn't it?"

"No, that's the name of the Catholic Church here. It was Saint Princess Joanna of Portugal."

Carly nodded. "My mistake. For some reason, I was thinking of Ursula from that cartoon movie, *The Little Mermaid*."

Julia chuckled. "I wonder why they chose Ursula for the villain's name in that movie. As a saint, Ursula is the patroness of education of schoolgirls. Maybe like the girl we found on the beach. Nothing to do with mermaids!"

"I hope Drew finds out who she is if she's not a Lejeune after all. Her parents have to be frantic. I know *I* would be."

"I'll forward this email to him. Maybe it'll shake up the cobwebs and get him to act."

∼

WEDNESDAY MORNING

The sun streamed into their guest bedroom with the promise of yet another glorious tropical day.

They padded into the kitchen where Rita was putting the final touches on a platter of food. She asked, "What plans do you have for today, ladies? The weather forecast for the morning is good, but there could be a squall later. You'll want to arrange your adventures accordingly." She poured two steaming cups of coffee and placed a platter of food on the small table where Antonio was already sitting.

Julia and Carly devoured the fresh mango and pineapple chunks that Rita had prepared. The thinly sliced deli ham and fresh brioche were a perfect complement to the fruit.

"Julia and I hope to snorkel today, somewhere," said Carly. "Anywhere!"

"And Noah invited us to watch the filming later today,"

said Julia. "The director has lined up some girls from a dance studio. I want to see what they're going to do with those Chinese-looking costumes and Asian shoes. Or maybe they're supposed to be Arabian, like in *Aladdin.*"

"Sounds interesting," said Antonio. "Rita and I are both busy today, so make yourself at home."

"I have another idea, Carly. What if we take a boat over to Tortola and talk to the police there? We could get permission from Drew first. Maybe he doesn't have time himself, and we could help with the leads he mentioned."

"You do mean the ferry, right?" Carly said, a little wary of her sister's boating skills.

"Too slow. I thought we could pop down to the marina and hire a boat for a couple of hours. It's a short hop over and back."

"You're cutting into my snorkeling time. And what about the movie set? I thought you were eager to check out the concubine scene."

Antonio broke in. "I have a powerboat that you can use. It's a nineteen-footer, and perfect for what you're proposing, Julia. I can call Mario to get it ready for you."

Julia squealed. "I like that idea." She turned to Carly. "If we go to Tortola first, considering the possible weather change this afternoon, we can get back in time to see the dancing girls and have snorkeling time, too, I think."

"You always try to squeeze in too many things in the same block of time. You do realize that, don't you?"

"Even if we only drop in on the movie set, we'll accomplish a lot. What do you say?"

Carly sighed. "It's not a terrible idea and I'd like to see Road Town anyway."

Antonio said, "I'll call Mario. The boat is named *Little Spirit.*"

"Thanks." Julia clapped her hands together. "This should be fun."

"Famous last words," said Carly.

CHAPTER

ELEVEN

J ulia took the wheel of the shiny powerboat, a Sea Ray SPX 190, after getting a quick lesson in operating it from Mario. He explained it was only thirteen miles to Road Town by sea and that he had topped off the gas tank that morning. He gave her a much-used nautical chart with an enlarged inset to help her with navigating into the harbor where Road Town was located once she got to Tortola.

Fortunately, Julia had been on several boat trips into the San Juan Islands off the coast of her home state, Washington, and the neighboring Gulf Islands of British Columbia in Canada. She enjoyed sailing with friends and had learned basic skills of watching land features for navigation purposes and keeping her eyes open for water hazards, such as reefs and buoys and other nautical oddities which can ruin one's day unexpectedly.

The ocean breeze cooled their faces and whipped their hair into "boat-dos" as they skimmed the azure water. Before long, Carly was picking out the coves and inlets on the southern shore of the main island of Tortola and matching them with the chart once they had motored around the tip of Beef Island.

"I had no idea it would be this much fun to be on the water," said Carly. "I was sure you would get us lost, or worse."

Julia made a face at her sister, then smiled and said, "As long as we can see land, it's pretty hard to get lost out here. If it were foggy, like it is some mornings in the San Juan Islands, I wouldn't want to be out here. It's really disorienting and getting turned around is dangerously easy."

Mario had given Julia instructions to tie up at the Moorings dock and to tell Sammy, his counterpart, that she had permission to use the boat. Antonio kept a couple of scooters at the Moorings Marina so Julia and Carly hopped on them and headed to the police station on Pickenin Road.

Drew had called ahead to his counterpart in Road Town so the sisters didn't have to waste time filling him in with the background. Police Chief Bernie Pickett was an affable, sandy-haired, middle-aged guy with piercing blue eyes.

Julia immediately thought of Peter O'Toole and his role in *Lawrence of Arabia*. Her mother had loved watching the old movie since her younger years. Julia's eyes welled with tears as she recalled enjoying it with her mom in those happy times before she became ill with cancer.

Chief Pickett picked up a manila folder and shared its contents with his guests. "You can see that we have a half-dozen open cases of missing women in the islands. And at least two of them fit the description of your Jane Doe."

"Have you had the families look at the pictures Chief Hawke sent over?" Julia asked as she studied the details of the other missing girls.

"Yes, but no one claims her yet. I was sure she would be one of these two," he said, pointing to two dark-haired girls. They were both pretty. The photos looked like high school yearbook pictures. "One of the families was sure she wasn't their daughter. I haven't been able to locate the other family although their last known address was here on Tortola. Frustrating." He sighed.

"We met a medicine woman yesterday who told us the girl was from the Lejeune family. Descendants of the Arawak."

Chief Pickett exclaimed, "That's the name of the other family that I haven't been able to locate. Did she say how she knew?"

Julia shook her head. "We didn't ask. I got the sense that she knew in some way that we wouldn't understand."

"I'm not much of a believer in spirits and all."

Julia smiled. "I get that. It's hard to understand that some people appear to have gifts such as extrasensory perception or telepathic skills that can't be explained in any logical way. I remember our mom having several premonitory dreams that came true."

Carly nodded, recalling their mother's telling of her experience.

"Another question for you, Chief," said Julia. "Has Chief Hawke—Drew—said anything about the drugs in the treasure chest that the movie crew dug up a couple of nights ago? Do you think the missing girls are related to those drugs?"

"Yes. He told me and sent some packets over. Given the brazen actions of today's drug czars, I wouldn't be surprised by just about anything. We simply can't patrol everything that goes on out on the ocean, or in the air. There are active cartels in the waters of Southeast Asia, off the western coast of Africa, and right here in God's country."

Julia nodded. "In addition to the land routes through Mexico and Central America."

"I sent the drug packets off for testing. Maybe we'll get

lucky and be able to pin them to one of our known trafficking rings."

"You can do that?" Julia's eyes widened.

"Almost. I like them to think we're close on their trail. It's only a matter of time and a lot of luck before we get a break-through."

"I wish you well," said Julia, standing to leave. "We need to get back to Spanish Town before the weather turns bad. Thanks for your time."

"Are you going to check out our little town while you're here?"

Julia shook her head. "Not today. Our host warned us that a squall that might be coming in, so we'd better head back before he starts to worry."

"Safe travels." He tipped an imaginary hat.

SAMMY PROMISED to take care of putting the scooters away after helping Julia and Carly cast off in the powerboat.

"Thank you! Ciao!" Julia yelled over the noise of the outboard motor.

"Carly, look at the chart and tell me how far it is from here to Dead Chest Island, please." Julia steered the boat at the maximum speed of five miles per hour out of the harbor toward the open water.

"We're not going there."

"Why not?"

"What about the weather that Antonio warned us about?"

"Look at the sky. The clouds are all behind us to the west. There's nothing straight ahead to worry about. It's only nine nautical miles to Dead Chest, and it's practically on the way back to Virgin Gorda. We can be there in about fifteen minutes."

"Why do you want to go there?"

"To look for buried treasure, of course." Julia grinned at her sister. "It'll only take a few extra minutes to swing by the island. It's only a half mile off Peter Island, so we'll be in sight of land the whole time."

"I don't like it, Julia." Carly crossed her arms and tapped her foot on the boat's carpeted floorboard.

"Trust me."

"I've heard that line before."

PICKING out the silhouette of the tiny island which was located just off the northeastern tip of Peter Island was difficult because of the boat's angle of travel until they were within the last mile or so.

"I see it," said Carly. "It looks tiny."

"It's not much more than sand that's built up on an old reef and a few palm trees that grew from random coconuts. That's what I read online." Julia slowed the boat speed and cruised along the isle's shoreline. She didn't see any mooring rings or other evidence that the island was used for routine anchoring. She doubted it could provide much protection from storms or winds from any direction because of its low profile and lack of suitable coves.

"Not much to see," said Carly. "Now can we please leave?"

"Yep. Let me see that chart again so I can check the coordinates for Spanish Town."

Julia idled the motor while she charted the straightforward course back to Virgin Gorda. "Got it. Let's go."

But when she pushed the throttle and started to go

forward, the engine died and the boat jerked to a stop, almost throwing Carly into the water.

"What happened? What are you doing?"

"Nothing. Let me try that again." Julia tried starting the engine again, but nothing happened when she turned the key except the sound of whirring. "I need to check the propeller. Maybe it's tangled and that's why I can't start the engine." Julia scrambled to the stern and peered into the shallow water.

"Carly, do you see that black button on the side panel next to the steering wheel that's labeled trim or maybe power trim? That will raise the motor so I can see what's going on."

Carly scanned the buttons and controls, knowing nothing about boating. "I see it. Now what?"

"Press it firmly."

Carly crossed the fingers of her left hand while she followed Julia's instruction. "Is it working?"

"Yes. Thanks. I can see the propeller but there's no seaweed." She groaned. "I'll try starting the engine again. Maybe I flooded it. You can put the motor back down."

"Hurry. I can see black clouds heading our way from the east."

"Roger that." Julia turned the ignition key again. Nothing happened but the unhappy sound of a dead engine. "We might be out of gas."

"How? Mario said the boat had a full tank. Now what?"

"Dang," said Julia. "Let's look around for some flares. They'll look kinda like sticks of dynamite that you see in cartoons. We can set one off and hope someone sees us from Peter Island. I don't know if there're any homes or hotels nearby, but we need to do something."

"I'm scared," Carly said as she began opening doors of the compartments in the cockpit.

"I know. Me too. But we're Finns and Finns have *sisu* and we can do this." Julia flashed a grim look at her sister.

"Found one," said Carly. "How do I set it off?"

"What kind is it? Look at the label. Is it a parachute flare?"

"Um, yes."

"Okay. Hold it in your left hand, pointing the top end away from the boat. Pull off the cap on the bottom, and you'll see a trigger mechanism of some kind."

"Okay. Cap is off. I see a cord to pull."

"Good. Aim the flare into the sky and pull that string down hard. You'll see a flare go up in the sky like a Roman candle. Remember those from Fourth of July fireworks? And then a red parachute will float down."

"And then what?"

"Cross your fingers and pray that someone sees it and comes to help."

"Yikes."

CHAPTER
TWELVE

Antonio checked the time again. He had been watching the gray clouds darken in the eastern sky and felt the air change as a squall threatened to drop its heavy load of rain at any moment. He picked up his cell and called the marina.

"Mario. Have you seen Julia and Carly yet? They should be back by now."

"No, boss. I'll call Sammy at Moorings and see what time they left Road Town."

"Good. Call me right back."

Antonio paced the floor in the small kitchen for the next several minutes, willing the phone to ring. He answered immediately when it did. "Yes, Mario. What did you learn?"

"Sammy said they left the dock about forty-five minutes ago. They should have arrived here by now."

"So where are they?"

"Should I take one of the other boats out and look for them?"

"Wait for me. I'll be there in ten."

"Yes, sir. I'll have the boat ready."

THE CLOUDS TURNED DARKER GRAY; Carly felt a few raindrops on her arms. "We should have brought another layer of clothes. This life vest isn't going to keep me dry."

Julia said as she checked the darkening sky, "I don't like the looks of those clouds. We won't have any protection from easterly winds in this location. I wonder if we should try to get over to Peter Island. It's only a mile away."

"Except the engine won't start."

"Oh, yeah. I don't suppose you saw any oars when you looked for a flare, did you?"

"This is a powerboat, not a rowboat, sis. I didn't see an anchor either. We're just bobbing in the water."

"The anchor should be in a compartment somewhere on the bow, but I don't really want to be sitting here in a storm, anyway," said Julia. "If we don't get rescued soon, I'll look for it so we don't float out any further." With a pair of binoculars she'd found in the lazarette she scoped out the shoreline of Peter Island. She squealed. "I see a boat coming around from the north end of that big cove in front of us."

"Should I send up another flare? There's one more right here."

"Yes. We need all the help we can get."

Carly successfully launched the second flare, aiming it where Julia pointed her finger.

"It looks like that boat is heading this way. Maybe he saw our flare." Julia put her hands together and closed her eyes. "Please, God. Let him be coming to help us."

Julia and Carly clung to each other in an attempt to stay warm as the rain began pelting them with gigantic pellets that felt like cold, wet bullets. Julia kept her eye on the approaching boat, which turned out to be a twenty-four-foot cabin cruiser. It seemed like forever but after another few moments it pulled up next to them from the western end of Dead Chest Island's southern shore.

One man called from the cockpit while a second man piloted the boat. "Can you use some help?"

Julia nodded vigorously. "Our engine won't start. We might be out of gas."

"Brace yourself while I toss you a line."

He threw a rope across the water from about seven feet away. Julia caught it and looped the end around one of the aft cleats. She saw a flash of silver at her feet as she cinched the line tight. She reached down to see what it was just as the man called out, "Throw me your bowline." She quickly pocketed the small item and pointed toward the line. "Grab it, Carly."

Carly scrambled to the bow and tossed the rope to the man's waiting arms. In a matter of minutes, he had attached a couple of bumpers on the port side of the larger cabin cruiser and had pulled the girls' boat next to the bigger one using the lines. He secured them and helped Julia and Carly crawl over to safety, after making sure Julia had left the ignition key in the off position.

"I'm Max. That's Ben at the wheel. Who are you?" He handed them each a proper weatherproof jacket, albeit on the large side.

"Julia. That's my sister Carly."

"Where are you going?"

"Back to Spanish Town. We are staying at a bed-and-breakfast, the Spirit of the Island, with Antonio and Rita Pacini. We got caught in the weather."

"No kidding. You two girls go below. Ben and I will tow you to Spanish Town. I'll call the harbormaster and let him know

I've got you. Someone is probably worried about you. At least, I hope they are." He smiled kindly as he closed the door.

~

ANTONIO AND MARIO left the marina in his yacht *Spirit* in the pouring rain. "Damn! I shouldn't have let the girls take the boat today. They don't know a thing about the weather down here."

Mario nodded. "Something must have happened, Boss. They had enough time to get back if they left Road Town when Sammy said they did."

Antonio grunted. "Keep your eyes open. They'll be hard to see in this rain."

"We should be able to pick them up on radar when we get close enough."

~

BEN JOINED the girls in the cabin about ten minutes later. He poured a couple of mugs of hot cocoa from a thermos jug. "My wife always sends me out with emergency cocoa," he said, grinning. "I have some brandy here also." He poured a bit of the caramel-colored liquor into each mug.

"Th-th-thanks," said Julia.

"It's n-n-nice," said Carly.

Ben sat across from the girls on one of the settees. "What were you doing at Dead Chest Island? I'm sure you realize that the days of finding buried treasure around here are long gone."

"My bad," said Julia. "We met some guys filming a pirate movie over on Virgin Gorda and they said they had shot some footage over there yesterday. I wanted to check it out."

"Didn't you check the weather before you headed out?"

"We knew there was a chance of a squall, but we thought we had enough time to beat it on our way back from Road Town." Julia looked at her sister. "Carly tried to stop me."

Carly nodded, daggers in her eyes as she glared at her sister.

"I didn't see any shopping bags," said Ben. "What were you doing in Road Town?"

Julia looked at Carly. "We went to the police station."

Ben furrowed his brows. "The police station? Why on earth ...?"

"It's kind of a long story," said Julia.

"And it sounds more stupid all the time," added Carly, still glaring at her sister.

"Hey." Ben stood back, shaking his hands in front of him. "I don't need to know. Let's just get you back before anyone misses you."

The cabin's intercom came to life with Max's voice.

"I've called the harbormaster. He's letting Antonio know that we've got the girls and that they're all right. He'll meet us at the marina. ETA twenty-two minutes."

"We have to go a little slower with your boat lashed on, not to mention this rough water," said Ben. "And it's going to be trickier to dock when we get back to Spanish Town. I'm going up to help Max. Make yourself at home." He saluted and was gone.

"I'm sure glad Max and Ben came along when they did," said Carly. "I was ready to commit mutiny."

"I don't blame you. I'm sorry I got us into this mess. I'll buy you dinner."

Carly shook her wet, blonde curls. "That's not going to cut it this time. I'll let you know what it's going to cost you."

Julia slumped back, and as she did her elbow touched a bump in her pocket. She reached into her pocket and held her hand open. Her mouth fell open. "Look what I found." A blue and silver harmonica was lying in her palm.

THE RAIN HAD LET up and the skies had lightened by the time they reached Spanish Town. Mario and Antonio took care of *Little Spirit* while Max and Ben talked with the harbormaster for a few minutes before heading back to Peter Island. Julia and Carly waved goodbye as *Rescue Me* motored out of the marina.

Julia faced the unwelcome task of telling Antonio why they had detoured on the way back from Road Town, and that the engine had died and wouldn't restart. She was properly admonished before Antonio enveloped both Julia and Carly in a big, warm hug.

"I'm glad you're safe after all that. Mario will take care of the boat and I will take you to Rita. She is worried sick over you, like a mother hen."

SNUGGLED in chairs with warm blankets after dinner, and fortified with more cocoa and brandy, Julia and Carly told Antonio and Rita about meeting Chief Pickett and learning more about girls missing from the islands.

"I wonder if any of the other girls met the same fate as our girl," said Julia.

"We need to give her a name. Jane Doe is so nobody," said Carly.

Julia bit the edge of her lip. "We could do that. How about Joanna, for the name of the saint on the pendant?"

"Or Ursula because she's the patron saint of girls."

Julia scoffed. "Nobody is named Ursula these days. Or

Joanna. How about Elizabeth? It's a pretty name."

"If you need another vote," said Rita, "I like Elizabeth. That was my niece's name."

"Was? Did something happen to her?" asked Julia.

Rita sighed and looked off in the distance. "She died of an overdose ten years ago. She was only eighteen. She had met some guys who promised her all kinds of things. Instead, she became addicted to the drugs that came with the promises. She refused to go to rehab. She said she could beat it by herself. Well, you can guess the rest."

Julia nodded. "Those habits are nearly impossible to break. I'm so sorry, Rita."

"It broke my sister's heart. She was depressed for a long time and only recently has been able to be more like her old self. I hope you find the drug dealer who killed this young girl —Elizabeth. I would love to see him rot in jail." She struck her fist on the table and left the room.

Silence and sadness hung in the air. The tropical squall had passed, leaving a clear sky. The sunset sent its soft rays into the comfortable room which was decorated with floral motifs and colorful tropical birds.

Antonio picked up his guitar and started plucking out a tune, initially unfamiliar to Julia's ears. The haunting melody eventually penetrated her brain, and she recognized the song from *Les Miserables*. Antonio was playing the song "Bring Him Home" but Julia thought perhaps he was playing it because of his wife's niece, to bring *her* home. Or maybe for this more recent victim.

Julia and Carly had three more days on the island. That gave them enough time to snorkel and lie on the beach, but would they find their murderer in that time? Julia knew in her heart that she couldn't stop looking. It wasn't in her DNA to give up on a puzzle.

CHAPTER
THIRTEEN

" I know better than to suggest going to the beach to snorkel because you're going to drag me along to play detective anyway." Carly finished drying her hair and plopped down in the Papasan chair. "Do you have any good ideas to figure this out?"

Julia pressed her lips together. "There are too many disconnects and not enough solid evidence. Even Chief Pickett hasn't been able to find her family, if she really is a Lejeune. If we could find them, we would have a better chance of connecting the dots."

"The local police haven't been successful. Why do you think you'll have any better luck?" Carly smoothed lotion onto her legs. "And do I have to remind you that it's not your problem?"

Julia smiled at her sister. "I know. But I feel lucky. We'll still make time to lie on the beach sometime today. Let's have some breakfast. I hear Rita and Antonio talking."

Sure enough, Rita was setting the table while Antonio

commanded the cooktop when the sisters waltzed into the sunlit kitchen.

"Good morning, my little ladybirds," said Antonio. "Please sit down and enjoy some coffee and papaya while I finish the breakfast casserole. It's an old family recipe and is quite delicious." He smiled as he stirred his creation in a cast-iron skillet on the stove.

"Smells good," said Julia. "I might have to take you home with me. I need a cook." She giggled.

"No way," said Carly. "I've got dibs."

Rita giggled from the doorway. "Excuse me, but I've got first dibs. Antonio, here's your phone. Mario needs to talk to you."

Rita took over at the stove while Antonio stepped away. Julia could hear muffled tones but no real words, although she could see Antonio's face had changed to an angry look when he turned back toward her.

"What is it?" Julia asked when he ended the call.

"Mario told me the gas tank was empty. He assured me it was full when you left. You should have been able to go miles and miles farther."

"Are you saying it was a deliberate action? Like someone siphoned the gas?" Julia shivered in the warm room.

"That, or punctured the gas line or tank to create a leak. Mario is calling Sammy at the marina on Tortola for more information." Antonio's face was grim. "Someone sabotaged one of my boats."

Carly's face was ashen. "That's scary. I knew I didn't like boats. That's one more reason to stay on land."

"I suppose it's possible that whoever did this was trying to thwart Carly and me," said Julia, looking at Antonio. "Since I was using the boat yesterday, not you."

He nodded slowly. "Maybe you girls are making somebody nervous."

"You make *me* nervous," said Carly to Julia.

Rita placed two plates on the table. The aroma was irresistible. "Eat your breakfast. You're safe here. Antonio and Mario will figure out what's going on."

JULIA AND CARLY lounged on the sun-dappled patio after breakfast. Carly was emailing her husband, Rob, while Julia tried to read the mystery she'd barely opened. She had finally finished reviewing the theater's bylaws. She held the blue and silver harmonica in one hand, being careful to use a tissue to preserve any fingerprints. She was having trouble concentrating and finally closed the book and picked up a notebook and pen. She made a list of the events that had happened in the short time she and Carly had been on the island.

"Okay, Carly. It's time to use our smart brain cells and figure out what's going on."

Carly groaned and pulled her feet under her on the chair. "Leave it to Drew and the police. My brain cells are on vacation."

Julia sniffed. "Your body is on vacation. Your brain cells are always on alert."

"Says who?"

"Says me. Listen to what I've got. Maybe our two brains can make sense of this. I've written this in chronological order, but it may not be correct, as we don't know certain background events." Julia began reading her list.

"We find Elizabeth and the pendant and shoe on the beach on Sunday."

"Our first mistake," said Carly.

"On Monday, we saw the pirate movie crew and the costumes that looked like what the victim was wearing."

"And met Noah," Carly said dreamily.

"Do you remember that he seemed a little antsy when I mentioned that we were going to talk to the police that day?"

"Not really. And so what?"

"Granted. Then we talked to Chief Hawke—I mean, Drew —and told him that we'd seen the look-alike costumes and shoe."

"Then we talked to that funny old priest." Carly giggled. "I didn't know priests wore normal looking clothes. I thought they always wore those robe thingies."

"That robe thingie is called an alb. They wear that when they're in the church for mass and funerals and other ceremonies. Priests are allowed to wear street clothes other times. But I know my friend, Father Scott, usually wears his black shirt and white collar when he's in public instead of what normal guys wear. Anyway, he told us that the pendant looked very old and hooked us up with the local diocesan office."

"And he said he didn't know the girl but that she could have been from another island, or not Catholic, or both."

"Right. And then we sent the pictures of the pendant to the antiquities shops in San Juan. That was after Antonio told us about people occasionally finding pirate treasure on the beaches in the islands."

"Was it the next day that we saw the pirate ship when we were at The Baths? And Noah showed up again?" asked Carly.

"Yes. Sometimes it seems like he's following us. More likely, you." Julia smiled at her sister, who possessed the powerful men-attracting pheromones. "And that was the same evening the pirates dug up the chest with the drugs and pirate loot."

"Or fake loot. And the matching shoe. And the police got

called in."

"And later Noah admitted to us that he'd seen our victim hanging around the movie set, even though he'd denied it earlier." Julia furrowed her brows. Her operating mantra was "joyful integrity" and she detested subterfuge.

"I think it was the next day that we went to Jost Van Dyke to Sidney's for that yummy lobster meal" said Carly.

"And we saw the pirate ship, or *a* pirate ship heading west from where we were. And then we went to Foxy's, and he said he didn't know anything about them except that they went back and forth. I got the sense he or Miguel knew more."

Carly said, "Yikes. That's a lot of events in one week. Or more accurately, four days."

Julia smiled at Carly's growing interest in following the threads of the mystery. "The next day we went back to Savannah Bay and heard those three guys talking. And saw the spirit woman by the rock."

"There could have been more than three guys, if there was someone who didn't talk. One of them played the harmonica, though rather poorly. And they talked about someone they referred to as 'boss.'"

"And she told us the girl's last name was Lejeune," Julia continued.

"And now we have that harmonica. Could it be the same one? Can it be tested for DNA or fingerprints?"

"Maybe, Carly. But if it's connected to those guys we heard, how did it end up on Antonio's boat?"

"None of those guys sounded like Antonio to me, or anyone we've met so far," said Carly.

"True," said Julia. "I hope he isn't involved in anything illegal." She sighed. "I can't forget that we saw a yacht passing by that resembled Antonio's out there. But like you said earlier, there are probably a lot of them out here."

"And later we ran into Noah again, or I should say, he ran into us. It's like he has radar." Carly giggled.

Julia shook her brunette bob. "I don't understand how guys seem to hone in on you. Maybe you were microchipped and don't know it."

"I don't do anything! You know that."

"I know. I have to tease you, though. Okay, Noah told us about Brock's plan to use dancers from a local dance studio for his concubine scene. And that they filmed scenes on Dead Chest Island without incident."

"Is that the day you got the reply from the antiquities shop in San Juan? And the news about the pendant?"

"And we decided to go to Road Town to talk to the chief there to see if one of the missing girls had the last name of Lejuene."

"There was no *we* in that decision. *You* talked Antonio into letting us take a boat there and we got into trouble with the propeller when *you* decided you had to go by Dead Chest Island. And the police chief hadn't been able to talk to anyone in the Lejeune family anyway."

"Yes, but he admitted that one of the missing girls was maybe from that family. He just couldn't locate the parents."

Julia's smartphone pinged with a new email message. "It's from Chief Pickett." She read it aloud: "'The crime lab has identified the drugs as cocaine and fentanyl. High quality. Not sure of origin. No definitive markers.' That's no surprise, but it is nice to have confirmation."

"It's so sad that Rita lost her niece to drugs," said Carly, following a big sigh.

"And it seems that someone is trying to prevent us from finding out the identity of our young lady."

"And who killed her," added Carly.

103

CHAPTER
FOURTEEN

A half hour later Julia's phone came to life again with Drew's number on the screen.

"Did you find someone from the Lejeune family?"

"No, but another girl is missing. Monique Duniec didn't come home after the movie shoot yesterday."

"Oh, no! Just a sec. I'm putting you on speaker so Carly can hear you. What do you know?"

"Mrs. Duniec said that her daughter and five other young girls from the dance studio were invited to the beach at South Sound. They were supposed to act like Chinese concubines for a scene or two. She said they were offered fifty dollars each for a couple of hours of work."

"Noah mentioned something about Brock lining that up," said Julia.

"They were picked up at the studio in the morning and the parents were told that they would be returning by two o'clock. But there were only five of the girls in the van when it showed up. Monique wasn't one of them."

"Surely one of the other girls would know what happened to Monique."

"They all said the same thing, that Monique left the beach with a young guy that they assumed was a boyfriend, but none of them recognized him."

"Doesn't she have a cell phone? Has she called her parents?"

"They said she has one but she's not answering it and hasn't called home. They're frantic, of course, as most parents would be. And they said she doesn't have a steady guy."

"Did the other girls say anything else?"

"One of them said the director—Mr. Stubby, she called him —was hopping mad because Monique was still wearing her costume. She was supposed to turn it in as soon as they were done."

Julia and Carly locked eyes as Julia asked, "How can we help?"

"I'm following up on the boat incident yesterday. I need to interview Mario and I've asked Chief Pickett in Road Town to talk to Sammy. I had hoped you and Carly would talk to your friend Noah about what happened yesterday at the beach."

"Why do you think he'll talk to us? Isn't this a police matter?"

"Yes, it is, but I suspect he'll tell you more than he would me, and my lone officer is tied up with a court case today."

"Carly is nodding that we can do that. First, we'll have to track him down. I don't know the shooting schedule."

"I'll forward the director's contact info to you. Call him and tell him I've asked you to help me. Let me know what you find out."

"Yes, sir. Oh, we found a harmonica on one of Antonio's boats that we thought could be checked for fingerprints. We'll bring it to the station later."

"Fine. Don't get your hopes up. A harmonica is a common diversion on boats. Plus, it might have been lying there a long time."

Julia turned to Carly as she pocketed her phone. "Well, it looks like we have an assignment today. Are you game?"

"Sure. Let's find Monique before she becomes another Elizabeth."

Julia and Carly briefed Antonio and Rita about Drew's request.

"That sounds safe enough," said Antonio. "Promise me you'll stay on the island today. I have enough gray hairs from the last escapade."

Julia smiled soberly. "Roger that. Although right now it doesn't appear that staying on the island kept Monique safe."

BROCK HAD HESITATED a moment before telling Julia they would be filming at Little Bay again. When they arrived Julia and Carly noted the familiar black SUVs in the parking area and parked next to the one closest to the sandy set. They walked by the costume and makeup tents without running into any guards. Noah was in full captain regalia, as was his under-study, Luke. There were no dancing girls on site. Several men dressed like pirate swabbies stood around waiting for Brock to finish talking to Noah, who nodded periodically.

Brock finally walked to his director's chair next to the videographers and yelled, "Action."

The sisters watched as Noah stood nose-to-nose with one of the pirates. They were yelling at each other as the other swabbies milled about behind their surrogate leader. The lead pirate was the scruffiest-looking of them all, with long, dark, scraggly hair (a wig?), a big, gold hoop earring in one ear, and a short-bladed sword in his right hand.

Their voices got louder and angrier. Soon the other pirates added their noisy grunts. The tension in the air felt disturbingly real.

"Cut!" Brock jumped up from his perch. "That was good. Now, Luke, I want you to step in for Noah. Pirates, keep grunting and moving around. Remember you're angry that your rum rations have been cut. I want to shoot some footage from behind Luke so I can see your faces."

Noah stepped off the sandy set and mopped his glistening brow with a cloth that was handed to him by a young man. Noah spotted the sisters, picked up a bottle of water and moved toward them, a big smile on his face.

"What a nice surprise to see you two lovely ladies! I thought you might show up here yesterday when we had the girls here for the shoot because you asked about the female costumes." He stopped smiling. "What's the matter? Did I say something wrong?"

"Can we move away from the others?" asked Julia. "We need to ask you some questions."

"Uh, sure. Let's go over to the striped tent. It's usually empty." Noah peeked into the tent to be sure they were alone, then motioned for them to join him.

"I want to stay outside so we can see if anyone approaches," said Julia.

"Okay. No one can hear us from here. What do you want to know?"

Julia glanced at the list of questions she and Carly had come up with after the conversation with Drew. "How many dancers were here yesterday?"

Noah furrowed his brow. "Five—no, six. Yes, six girls."

"Okay. What exactly did they do while they were here? What was the scene setup?"

"Brock had Luke and me lounging in the shade of some palm trees. The dancers were dressed in those kimono-like things and were waving big fans over our heads, like they were cooling us off."

"All six of them?"

"Well, not all at once. They took turns, two at a time. I think Brock was looking for the cutest ones, but he didn't say that, of course." Noah chuckled and took a swig of his water. "He told us earlier he was paying them all the same but that he could cut out whatever he didn't like when they did the film editing at the studio."

"Okay. What else did they do?"

Noah looked away for a moment. "They walked around the other pirates like they were flirting, like they were trying to decide which one they liked the best."

"Did you notice any of the dancers in particular?"

"I'm not sure what you mean." Noah stood a little straighter. "They were just young girls prancing around in costume."

"So none of them stood out to you?"

"No, I don't think so." He frowned. "These are strange questions."

"I only have a couple more," said Julia. "Were there any guys that you didn't recognize hanging around while the girls were here?"

Noah shook his head, then paused and said, "Yes, there was a dude in black street clothes standing near one of the guards. I figured he was a local who wanted to watch what was going on, and security made him stay back."

"Did you notice when he left?"

"No. Brock called me over to reshoot the dueling scene right after the dancers were done. I didn't pay attention to him after that."

"Would you recognize him if you saw him again?"

Noah took a step back, his eyes narrowed. "What's going on?"

Julia looked at Carly with a raised eyebrow, then went ahead when Carly nodded. "One of the girls, Monique, didn't get home. There were only five girls in the van when it returned to the dance studio. The other girls told the police that Monique left with a guy. They thought he was her boyfriend, but her parents said she doesn't have one."

Noah's face paled. "Oh, brother. Now I get it. You're wondering if the guy standing next to the guard might have been the same one?"

"It sounds like a possibility. Can you point out which guard I should talk to?"

"Sure," said Noah. "Wait here a moment." He walked to the perimeter of the movie set where a couple of the security guys were standing. He talked to them briefly, then walked to the other side of the set where two other men stood. He had another brief conversation, ending with the men shaking their heads.

"None of them have seen that guy today. The guard who reportedly saw that guy hanging around was a substitute for one of the regulars from the local security company. They didn't know his name, but you could probably get it from the security office."

"Thanks, Noah. Carly and I will pass the info on to Chief Hawke. If you think of anything else, please let us know." Julia gave him a business card with her contact info.

Julia and Carly walked silently to their scooters.

Carly said solemnly, "Another missing girl and she was wearing that same costume."

Julia nodded as she straddled her ride. "I can't help but think this is connected to the first girl somehow. Let's go back to the house. We've got our work cut out for us if we're going to find Monique and get her home."

CHAPTER

FIFTEEN

J ulia and Carly lingered at the table with Antonio and Rita. They had shared their discovery from the movie set as well as other bits of information they thought might be evidence. The four of them were discussing how the pieces of the puzzle might fit together.

Julia jumped when her cell phone vibrated in her pocket. Drew's number lit up the screen. "What did you find out?" she asked before he could ask her the same question.

"Sammy, the main guy at Moorings in Road Town, said he didn't notice anything going on with *Little Spirit* while it was tied up there. He had a busy afternoon with charter sails going in and out and also had a new dock hand he was training. He said it was possible that someone could have siphoned gas from the boat or punctured the line and he wouldn't have noticed."

"That's a worry," said Julia. "Has this kind of thing happened before?"

"He told me it was a first for him. He also said the new dock hand didn't show up today although he was scheduled to work. He's mad because it left him short-staffed on a busy day."

"Did he have a name for the dock hand? Or a description?"

"I didn't get that info but I can call back. Why? What did *you* find out?"

"It might not be anything, but Noah, the actor we've met, said an unfamiliar young guy was hanging around the set yesterday when the dancers were there. He disappeared at some point."

"And you're wondering if he's the guy Monique left with?"

"Correct."

"Well, it's hard to imagine that this guy could have been in Road Town messing with your boat and at the movie set at the same time."

"I hadn't thought of that," said Julia. "Just a sec. Carly is trying to tell me something."

Carly said, "Noah also told us that one of the security guards was a substitute and he was the guard who the unknown guy was talking to. Maybe they're in on whatever is going on."

"I heard that," said Drew. "I'll send my assistant chief, Lenny, to the security company to check that out."

"Has there been any word from Monique?"

"Not yet. I've got volunteers going door to door and making phone calls. As you can imagine, her parents are frantic. They've talked to all of her friends and classmates. No one knows of her talking about a boyfriend so far."

"Did you find out anything about the jewels in that pirate chest? I assume you know from Chief Pickett that the drugs tested out as cocaine and fentanyl, as he suspected."

"I was going to tell you but Vern, Chief Pickett, said he'd already told you. Anyway, the jeweler in Road Town consulted with someone in San Juan. He said it's possible that some of the jewels are old, because they look like something from the fifteenth or sixteenth century, but they haven't been evaluated in person by a gemologist."

"Like the pendant we found on the first girl?"

"Exactly. I've sent out memos to police departments in the other Caribbean islands asking about individual pieces of pirate booty showing up recently."

"You might also check with antiquities stores and museums and ask if they have any knowledge, or if they've been contacted."

"Great idea. I'll ask Vern to take care of that."

"Is there something I can do to help?"

"I can't think of anything, Julia. Just keep your eyes and ears on alert."

"Is it okay if I tell Antonio and Rita about all this? Is any of it top secret?"

"None of what I've told you is sensitive information, if that's what you mean," Drew replied. "I trust Antonio and Rita to keep anything you tell them close to their chests. I've known them a long time."

JULIA SETTLED in her chair and shared with the others what the police chief had said. "I can't help wondering what we're missing. There has to be something that would connect all the pieces, if we could only find it." She nibbled on one of the spice coconut bars Rita had made for dessert. "Yum. Another new favorite."

"I have connections through my IT background if you can steer me in a specific direction," said Antonio.

"Are you able to do any research on the drug trade around

here?" asked Julia. "It would help to know who the lynchpins are and what methods they use."

Antonio grinned. "I know some guys in the business. It may take a few hours. I'll have to go to my office where I have more computer power."

Julia looked up. "You have an office somewhere? This isn't all you do?"

He laughed. "Having this small bed-and-breakfast is what Rita and I do for fun. I made my fortune inventing and selling a powerful app that caught the eye of a major company. They paid me enough money that I can work less hard and continue to play at making more inventions. In fact, I do some consulting work for them. I evaluate other potential acquisitions that may be useful to them."

"That explains some things," said Julia.

Antonio looked at her with narrowed eyes. "Were you wondering if I made my money by some nefarious means?"

Julia turned pink. "It crossed my mind."

Antonio shook his head and put his hands on his hips. "Wait till my DEA friends hear this one." He chuckled, then kissed Rita goodbye and promised to call if he learned something helpful as he headed out the door.

"You and your suspicious mind," said Carly, rolling her eyes.

Rita picked up the dishes from the table and said, "Don't worry. Antonio doesn't take it personally. He has thick skin from his earlier days."

ALONE AGAIN, Carly checked her email while Julia read over the list of questions she'd asked Noah.

"Rob says 'hi' and wants to know if we've figured out our mystery yet."

"Tell him 'hello' for me."

"Sure thing. By the way, you haven't mentioned Josh at all this week. Are you staying in touch, or is that a bad question?"

Julia smiled as she thought of the long-distance relationship with her east coast friend. "We usually email back and forth about once a week. He knows I'm here on vacation and that wi-fi could be iffy."

"Is he still considering a visit to Portland? Or was it Seattle?"

"His company hasn't made a decision about a west coast site, but he's talking about meeting me somewhere in the spring."

"Not in Paris, I hope."

"Definitely not Paris. And maybe it will be a real vacation without business meetings attached."

"That would be nice."

"If you're done with your email, how about going out and seeing what's going on? Maybe we could run into Noah again." Julia ducked as Carly pretended to throw a pillow at her.

Promising to be back before dinner, the sisters hopped on the scooters and headed for the east side of the island, where they figured Noah would still be filming.

"Why do you want to go to the movie set again?" Carly asked while walking down the sandy trail. "Do you suspect him of something?"

"No, not Noah. At least, I don't think I suspect him."

"That doesn't even make sense the way you said it."

"What I mean is that both of the girls appear to be

connected to the movie set—either directly, in the case of Monique, or indirectly, for Elizabeth. There has to be someone who knows something but isn't talking."

"What about the girl and guy who were in the makeup tent that day? We've never seen them again, but Noah has mentioned having to get made-up at least a couple of times."

"Good thought. I wonder if they're local or if Brock brought them with him from wherever his studio is."

"It would be an extra expense to bring anyone other than the necessary crew all the way from Hollywood, if that's where he's based."

"They could be from anywhere, really. This is a resort island and I'm sure the lodging and food aren't cheap." Julia stopped walking just before they reached the blue-striped cabana where they'd waited their first time on the set. "Let's talk to the makeup people first. You can flirt with the guy— Matt, I think his name was—while I play twenty questions with the girl."

"Her name was Lissa," said Carly. "I remember because I thought she left off the first part of it—like it should be Alissa."

"It probably *is* Alissa or Melissa, but she goes by a nickname."

LISSA WAS SITTING on a high stool scrolling through TikTok when Julia asked if she could pose a few questions about the makeup she did for the dance studio girls. She came to life as she described how she first applied the different layers and shades of foundation to create a paler skin tone. Then she had used black eyeliner and mascara to maximize the eyes, making them appear more almond-shaped. Brock had wanted them to resemble geisha girls.

"I thought he wanted them to be Chinese concubines?" asked Julia.

Lissa snickered. "I'm not sure he knows the difference."

"Maybe not. Do you remember any of their names? Did you do the makeup for all of them?"

"Matt and I each did three of the girls. Um ... there was a Sierra, an Annalee, and a Nikki in my group. I don't know who he had."

"Thanks. Was there anything that you noticed about any of your girls? Like were they nervous, or scared, or did they say anything that struck you as unusual?"

"They were all dumbstruck and excited. They didn't act like they were scared at all. Nikki mentioned how she hoped to be in the real movies someday, as if this weren't real," she scoffed.

"Anything else?" asked Julia.

"I can't think of anything." Lissa scrutinized Julia's face. "Do you want me to do your makeup while you're here? I could give you a great smoky eye look."

Julia gave Lissa a half smile as she backed out of the tent. "Thanks, but I've still got work to do this afternoon. Oh, I forgot to ask if you're from here or Hollywood."

Lissa laughed. "Definitely not from Hollywood. Only in my dreams. I work for a studio in San Juan. They farmed Matt and me out for this gig."

Carly was sitting in Matt's makeup chair when Julia walked over to join them. She blushed when she noticed Julia looking over Matt's shoulder. "Matt's demonstrating the makeup he did for the dancers," she explained.

"I see. You're looking like a real geisha girl, except your blonde curls don't fit the image."

"Matt said they had wigs for us blondies."

"Of course. Did you find out anything helpful? Like the girls' names?"

"He said he made-up three girls. One of them was Monique —the prettiest one, he said. The other two were Sonja and Edita. Is that right, Matt?"

Matt smiled and continued to work on Carly's makeup as she answered the questions on his behalf.

"Did he have any comments about how they interacted with the crew or the actors?"

"He said he didn't notice anything. Once the girls left the makeup tent, he went back to reading his email and stuff like that."

While Julia and Carly continued to chat, Matt selected a wig that was styled in the typical geisha style, including a topknot with a fancy comb. Once he placed it on Carly's head, the transformation from a blonde American to a Japanese geisha was amazing. The only feature Julia recognized was Carly's unique eye color, which was somewhere between green and hazel, depending on what color she was wearing or the lighting.

"Oh my. You'd fool our own mother looking like that."

"Shall we check it out on Noah?" Carly admired her look in the mirror and grinned.

Julia tilted her head and raised her eyebrows. "He might think he's seeing a ghost."

CHAPTER
SIXTEEN

J ulia, looking like her normal self, and Carly, fully
costumed and made-up, traipsed through the sand to
the filming set. Brock was giving instruction to the
motley band of pirates. Several were lounging in raggedy
hammocks set up between palm trees. A couple more were
decanting liquid (the daily rum ration?) from an old cask that
had been set up on a makeshift deck. Noah and his stand-in,
Luke, were waiting in the shade with the film crew until Brock
was ready for them.

Julia noted that sometimes Luke's costume was identical to
Noah's and other times he was dressed like a different person,
as he was today. She guessed he was playing a separate character at times when he wasn't standing in as Noah's captain
character. Maybe for dangerous scenes involving weapons,
such as when the pirates had pretended to be angry a day or
two earlier. She had read about the occasional accidental
deaths that occurred on movie sets, like when a presumably
unloaded gun killed someone.

Carly sidled up to Noah without saying a word. It was a

long moment before he noticed someone standing next to him. He jumped when he turned and saw Carly. His face went ashen and his jaw dropped open. "Where did you come from? I-I-I thought you disappeared yesterday?" he stammered.

Carly laughed. "It's *me*, Carly. You should have seen the look on your face, Noah. Who did you think I was?"

"You look like the girl who turned up missing. Monique. I thought I was seeing a ghost."

Julia stepped forward and said, "I thought you didn't know one girl from another."

Noah's color had returned. "I didn't know all their names, but Monique seemed more sophisticated than the others. She stood out, even with all of them dressed and made-up the same."

"How did you know her name?" Julia asked, eyebrows furrowed.

"I asked. I thought it might make her feel more comfortable since she was supposed to act like she was special to me. And she was pretty. I wanted to know who she was."

"And you're sure you haven't seen her since she left after the filming was done?"

"Hey, yeah." Noah held up his hands and stepped back. "I'm sure. I'd love to find out that she's okay, wherever she is."

"Okay," said Julia. "Did she say anything at all that could help locate her? Like, was she meeting someone later?"

"Not to me. I swear I didn't pay attention to any of the girls once we were done filming that scene. I had to change into another costume right away, so I didn't see them leave."

Julia turned to face Luke, who stood a few feet away. "What about you? Did you notice or see something?"

Luke didn't seem surprised by the question and didn't flinch. He snorted. "They were just a bunch of high school girls playing dress-up. When we were done with that little charade, I left to change costumes, same as Noah. End of story."

Brock yelled at Noah and Luke to move over to the set for the next scene.

"I gotta go play pirates," said Noah, "but please let me know if you learn anything. I'll do anything I can to help find her."

"Thanks. The police are doing their best. They hope to find her alive, which means they must find her quickly. It's already been twenty-four hours."

Julia and Carly returned the costume and wig, and Carly had Matt remove her makeup, but not before Julia took some photos for Carly to send to her husband and maybe post on Facebook.

"Did you notice Luke's reaction to the question about Monique?" asked Julia as they returned to their scooters.

"Yeah. I mean, they all know now that a girl is missing. And to be so dismissive about it? It seemed like he was acting."

"Or guilty because he knows something."

"I don't see how *he* could have spirited her away. He had to shoot another scene right away."

Julia screwed up her face. "He could have had help. There's still the mysterious guy that Monique supposedly left with. Maybe Luke had arranged something with him."

"But why?" Carly started her scooter and turned back toward the bed-and-breakfast with Julia following.

Julia slurped the last of her mango sorbet and sipped on the crispy-cold pinot grigio that Antonio had poured for an afternoon happy hour. "Where do you suppose Monique is hiding?" she asked. "Or perhaps it's more correct to say, 'being hidden.' I don't see her running off by herself, unless she has a horrible home life."

"We know her family a little bit," said Rita. "Her mother seems nice and has raised two other girls. They were about eight and ten years older than Monique."

"Is there a different father?" asked Julia. "That's a lot of years between children."

Rita laughed. "Monique was that 'bonus' child, as we say. I am sure she was very much loved."

"Sometimes that isn't enough," said Carly. "I can think of one of my friends growing up who was the youngest by ten years. She thought her parents were stricter with her and were old and stodgy compared to her friends' younger parents."

Julia tucked her feet under her on the chair. "I wonder if she left of her own volition, or if she was shanghaied herself. I can't help but think she was forced to go with someone. Otherwise, I think she would have called her parents. Maybe she can't call home because she's being held somewhere."

"And they probably took her phone away," said Carly. "I feel so bad for her."

Julia rested her chin on her hands, elbows on the table. "Antonio, where on the island would it be possible to hide someone? I mean other than a house or a hotel."

"Despite the island being small, at about eight square miles, there's still a lot of tropical forest where someone could be hiding."

"Like that spirit woman," said Carly. "She came out of nowhere. Maybe she lives in the forest."

Antonio smiled. "Yes, like the descendants of the Arawak or Caribe, who were the early inhabitants here." He glanced at Rita. "I understand there's a small tribe that lives somewhere deep in the forest. There are also a few abandoned ruins, such as the copper mines, that have the potential for hiding someone."

"She could have been taken to one of the other islands," said Julia. "Then she would be as hard to find as that proverbial needle."

"We can only hope she's still on Virgin Gorda," said Antonio.

"Is there a search and rescue organization on the island?" Julia knew only too well how difficult it would be to cover even eight square miles if Monique was being hidden in the forest.

"Yes, in a manner of speaking. Each neighborhood has a team leader who contacts the other members in his or her immediate area. It's somewhat primitive but has proven effective a couple of times when young kids have wandered off."

"How can we help?" asked Julia. "I can't just sit here waiting."

"The police are doing everything they can, Julia," Antonio replied. "I know you want to find Monique, but where would you look that hasn't already been searched?"

Julia flung her head back for a moment and sighed. She suddenly sat up straight again. "What if we tried talking to the girls at the dance studio? They might tell us something that they wouldn't tell the police."

"Or may have remembered a detail that could be helpful," added Carly.

Julia checked the time. "It's almost four. Dance studios are usually open at this time for classes after school. Maybe good karma will be with us."

CHAPTER
SEVENTEEN

The dance studio was bustling with activity. Youngsters from about age four to mid-teens milled about in a large room that served as a waiting area. Half of them had donned black leotards and ballet shoes. Others wore gymnastic-type clothes with flexible, soft-soled shoes. Julia peeked into one of the classrooms and saw six girls *en pointe* dancing to music from Tchaikovsky's *Nutcracker Suite*. She snapped a couple of photos of them as they flitted through a couple of moves, then held position until they were instructed to restart the sequence.

"I'll bet those are the girls who were at the filming on Wednesday," Julia whispered to Carly.

"Why did you take pictures?"

Julia raised a shoulder. "Maybe they'll help if Drew or you and I have to talk to the movie crew again."

"I guess that's a good idea," said Carly. "Let's find the manager and get permission to talk to them when they finish class."

The door to the office was closed and locked but through

the door's window, Julia saw a woman at a copier machine in the back of the room. She knocked. The woman turned her head and nodded. As she opened the door, she ran a hand through the stray hairs of her longish, auburn hair which had been pulled into a loose ponytail. She appeared to be in her late thirties or early forties, with a body fit for classical ballet. She wore a frazzled smile.

"Hi. I'm Sally Ritchie, the owner. How can I help you?"

Julia introduced herself and Carly and explained why they were there.

"But the students already talked to that police officer who was here yesterday. What else could they possibly tell you?"

"We were hoping one of them might remember a detail or two that they hadn't recalled the first time. Or maybe they'll be more willing to talk to us than to uniformed police officers." Julia smiled hopefully.

Ms. Ritchie pressed her lips together. "Well, all right. Although I hate to put them through any more trauma. They're already stressed over Monique not being here. They all looked up to her."

"Thanks so much," said Julia. "We appreciate the opportunity."

"Their class ends in ten more minutes. I'll have them meet you in the small classroom on the left at the end of the hall." She pointed to the hallway. "You can wait in there if you like."

Julia and Carly admired the dozens of photographs of dancers hanging on the walls as they strolled to the assigned room. There were ballerinas of all ages, tap dancers, and gymnasts. A handful of studio shots of famous dancers also hung in the hallway gallery, presumably placed there to inspire the students to pursue their own greatness.

Julia and Carly sat on a couple of tall stools in the class-room to wait. A few minutes later six young girls who appeared to be in their early- to mid-teens filed in and stood in a cluster in front of the sisters. None of them smiled. A couple of them sniffled.

"Hi," said Julia. "Thank you for coming in here. My name is Julia, and this is my sister Carly." Carly bounced up and curtsied, hair bouncing, a smile dancing on her face. "We're helping the police find your friend, Monique, and we'd like to ask you a few questions."

The girls looked at Julia, eyes wide.

Julia smiled kindly. "I know one of the police officers has already debriefed you, but often people remember more details a day or two later."

A couple of girls nodded.

"As I understand it, six of you went by van to the beach where they're shooting a pirate movie."

Nods all around.

"And Monique didn't get in the van when it was time to come back."

More nods, most eyes not meeting Julia's.

"There are six of you here so one of you must have stayed behind that day." Julia looked at each of the faces. "Which one are you?"

A petite, dark-haired girl raised her hand. "I couldn't go because I had to babysit my little brother after school." She started to cry. "I miss Monique."

Carly reached out and put her arm around the young dancer.

"Which one of you can tell me what happened when you were told you were done and could leave?" Julia looked at each of the girls.

The tallest of the six raised her hand. "We were in two groups of three. Monique and Edita were with me. I'm Sonja. We danced around those men and had to pretend we were flirting. It was hard because they were acting gross and making goo-goo eyes at us. We had to do it five or six times before the director, Mr. Hughes, said it was good enough."

"Okay. Did the same thing happen with the other three dancers?"

A slender girl with dark skin answered. "I'm Sierra. Annalee and Nikki and I did the same thing. I could hardly wait to be done." She hugged herself and shuddered. Two other girls, presumably Annalee and Nikki, nodded their heads vigorously.

"When did you notice that Monique wasn't with you?"

The girls looked at each other. Sonja answered for all of them, as though an invisible agreement had been reached. "We didn't notice she wasn't with us until we were walking back to the van after leaving our costumes and wigs with the makeup people."

"Who saw her leave the area with a guy? That's what Chief Hawke said the police officer was told."

More looks between the dancers. "No one actually saw her leave," said Sierra. "But I saw her talking to a guy who was hanging out near the security guards. We figured she left with him when we didn't see her in the van."

"Do any of you know who that was?"

Most of the girls shook their heads.

"No, ma'am," Sonja answered without looking at the other dancers. "None of us have ever seen him before."

"Okay," said Julia. "Thank you for staying after class to answer questions. I'm going to leave my business card with Ms. Ritchie. If any of you think of anything else, or want to call me, you can get my number from her."

The dancers left the room quickly, as though it had suddenly become too cold or they had remembered an important engagement.

Julia pursed her lips. "I have the distinct feeling that one of them knows something."

Carly nodded. "And is sworn not to tell."

"Sonja did most of the talking. I'll ask Ms. Ritchie for her phone number. It might be helpful to talk to her without the others."

JULIA CHECKED the time as they mounted their scooters. "It's not quite five. What about going down to the marina? I want to ask Mario if he knows of anyone who plays the harmonica,"

Carly groaned. "That could be a lot of people."

"I only care about the one who left that harmonica in Antonio's boat."

"Right. What about taking it to Drew at the police station? We talked about having it checked for DNA or fingerprints."

"Good idea. We have time to go to both places. Let's start with Drew, because he probably goes home before Mario does."

JULIA AND CARLY were ushered directly to the police chief's office, where Drew was on the phone. He turned his back to them while finishing the call.

Drew sighed and shook his head when he ended the conversation. "That was one of the lead searchers," he said to his visitors. "None of the teams have found any sign of Monique. I'm sure you know that the longer we go without finding her, the greater the chance we won't find her alive."

The sisters nodded gravely.

"Is there any way to be certain she's still on the island?"

asked Julia. "Have you checked at the marina? I'll assume you've checked the ferry already."

"No, yes, and yes," said Drew. "We can't know for sure if she's on the island, but I hope she is. We asked around at the marina. And no one on the ferry or at the ticket office recognized her photo, but she could have been in the trunk of a car or back of a van, unfortunately."

"I hadn't thought of that," said Julia. "The reason we stopped by today is to give you this harmonica that we found on Antonio's boat. We don't know if it's important but maybe it could be checked for fingerprints?" She handed it, safely protected from extraneous prints in a ziplock bag, to the police chief. "We thought we'd run down to the marina and talk to Mario, because we found it on Antonio's boat. Maybe he knows of a harmonica player amongst the dockhands."

Drew chuckled. "Let me handle that. I want to ask him about the gas situation anyway." He examined the harmonica briefly and said, "I don't know if the lab will find anything useful if it's been lying around, but it's worth a try. Maybe we'll get a real lead. Thanks." He produced an evidence bag from a drawer and labeled it before inserting the harmonica.

"What about leads from the jewelry? Anything new there?" asked Julia.

Drew's face lit up briefly. "Yes, as a matter of fact, an antiquities collector in San Juan responded to an inquiry that Chief Pickett in Road Town had sent out. He said he had been contacted by a man who wanted to show him fifteenth- and sixteenth-century jewelry and other collectibles."

"Maybe that's connected to the necklace that we found on the dead girl," said Julia.

"I agree with you on that. Unfortunately, the man wouldn't give the dealer any identification or contact information and Mr. Perez, the dealer, turned him down before he had seen the email from our department. Mr. Perez is well aware of illegal trafficking and didn't want to have any part of it. If he had known about our situation he would have set up a meeting with the man. Unfortunately, it's a dead-end for now."

"Maybe that guy will contact another dealer," said Julia, "and he can set up a sting now that the collectors have been alerted."

Drew nodded, a grim smile on his face. "We can only hope. There are many collectors out there who don't care about, or ignore, the provenance of this kind of treasure. And they're all over the world. I'm afraid we may have lost our best chance at trapping this unscrupulous ring."

A cloud of gloom hung in the air for a moment, then Julia told Drew what they'd learned from the dancers, and of her suspicion that Sonja knew something more. "I have her phone number. Do you mind if I call her?"

Drew rested his head on his open hand, elbow on the desk. His face sagged, etched with worry. "Great. Tell her you have my permission to ask questions if she hesitates."

EIGHTEEN

I n the parking lot where they'd left the scooters, they briefly discussed making a run to the site of the abandoned copper mine. Julia couldn't shake the sense that her unconscious mind was telling her to check it out, but Carly's argument that Rita had told them to be home for dinner by six kept her from heading in that direction. And she wasn't sure she wanted to be out there once the sun set.

"We'll have all day tomorrow to go there, Julia," said Carly.

Julia smiled glumly. "Every hour that we don't find Monique is an hour that we don't get back."

"I'm sure Drew has already had it checked out," said Carly. "He mentioned it when we asked about search parties."

Julia started to nod, then paused. "We were having that conversation with Antonio, not Drew. Remember?"

"You're right," said Carly. "But we can still call Drew and ask him if his men have been there. We still need to call Sonja when we get back to the house. She could have a hot date tonight so we should call her as soon as we can."

Rita had prepared a lovely dinner of prawns sautéed in garlic butter. They were accompanied by a green salad, rice pilaf and fresh rolls.

Though the food was tasty and the sun was streaming through the palms onto the patio, a sense of gloom hung in the air. Rita finally asked, "Is there something wrong? You two have hardly said a word and usually you chatter like those silly birds at sunset."

Julia said, "Oh, I'm sorry, Rita. The food is delicious as usual. I'm sad because we're leaving in a couple of days and we —I mean the police—still haven't found the dead girl's parents or Monique."

Carly explained, "Julia isn't happy until she ties up all the loose ends. Even if this is not her problem to solve." She narrowed her eyes at her sister. "Drew will stay on top of it after we leave, I'm sure."

Antonio spoke up, "Of course, he will. He's very good at what he does. Don't worry Julia. The whole island cares about finding Monique."

Julia took a swallow of her wine and dabbed at her lips. "Everything you say is true, but I can't help feeling that we should at least try to find Monique."

"Let's call Drew and Sonja as we planned, Julia," said Carly. "Maybe he knows something new."

"Since we talked to him a couple of hours ago? Ha! But you're right. Let's make those calls." She and Carly cleared their places at the table. "Thanks for dinner. We'll be in our room if you need us."

"SHALL I call Drew first or Sonja?" Julia asked once they were alone.

"Drew. Then we'll know if the copper mine area has been searched, and that's what we've been worried about today."

"I agree." Julia reached Drew on the second ring. She thought briefly of all the calls she received when she was on call for her clinic team and wondered if Drew wanted to throw his phone into the nearest body of water as she did sometimes. She smiled when she heard his voice. "Hi, Drew. Julia and Carly here. You're on speaker mode so she can hear you. Sorry to have to call again but we wondered if the search teams went to the copper mine. Antonio mentioned that it was one of the places he would think of if he were hiding someone."

"That's happened before, in case you didn't know. And, yes, that's one of the first places we looked. If you have a minute, I have some news about the other girl that I can share."

Julia sat up straight and glanced at her sister. "What is it? Did you find her parents?"

"They came into the office late today to report her missing. They had been visiting family members in Puerto Rico and didn't realize we were trying to contact them until they listened to my message on their phone after returning. They confirmed her identity from the photos you had taken."

"Oh my gosh! They must be devastated. Did they say anything else?"

"Her father said she had been acting strange lately, like coming home late after school, and talking a lot on the phone to some guy that she said she'd met at the beach."

"Did he have a name for the guy?"

"Unfortunately, no. She—Lorena, the daughter—was very secretive about who he might be. But they didn't think he was a local kid."

"Did you tell them about the drugs causing her death?"

"Not yet. I just couldn't do it. When her body returns from Tortola, we'll go over the autopsy report together. By then, they'll have had some time to get used to the idea that she's gone."

"That's one of the things I hate about our jobs," said Julia. "It's never easy to have to give bad news to families."

"Agreed. I showed them the photo of the pendant. The mother said her daughter had been wearing it recently. Lorena had said that the new boyfriend had given it to her."

"That's interesting. I wonder how he obtained it. It makes me wonder if he has anything to do with that chest of drugs and jewels that the pirates dug up earlier this week."

"I had the same thought," said Drew. "It would sure be nice to find the missing link that ties all this together."

"If—I mean, *when*—we find Monique, hopefully she can provide some missing details."

"I'll keep you posted," said Drew.

JULIA LOOKED OUT THE WINDOW. The sun had set but it was still dusk. The moon was high in the sky.

"Sis, are you game to go out to the copper mine now? The moon doesn't set until nine thirty and it looks like we have enough light to see. And we can take flashlights."

"Are you crazy?"

Julia shook her head. "When I lived in Dallas we had an annual Hobie Cat race by the light of the full moon in July or August. It was amazing how well we could see with the moon's reflection shining on the water. We usually didn't have much wind, but it was always a beautiful evening. Tonight's moon reminds me of a night like that."

Carly let out a big sigh. "Well, I better go with you before you sneak out of here alone. We don't need another missing person."

CHAPTER
NINETEEN

The moon gave off enough light to illuminate the roads and trails to the copper mine national park, just as Julia had predicted it might. The parking lot was empty of any vehicles this late in the evening. Not a breath of wind stirred the air. An occasional horn, perhaps from a boat on the water somewhere, penetrated the quiet stillness.

She and Carly decided to hide their scooters behind a large boulder to avoid advertising their presence in case of unexpected company. It had crossed Julia's mind that the locals might use the lonely site for late-night trysts.

They walked quietly to the rocky stacks that stood sentry at the old mine.

"I don't see how anyone could be hidden here," said Carly. "There's nothing here but these few walls and the rocky columns and it's all open to the elements." She stood between the parallel stacks of rocks and held her hands out, palms up.

"I remember reading that there are remnants of the shafts that went underground, and even under the water," said Julia.

"Maybe, but how would you get into them?" Carly looked

around at the rocks and rubble at her feet. "I don't see anything that resembles a door or window here."

"Let's walk around and see if there's anything lower along the cliff," said Julia as she turned to survey the cliffside between them and the Atlantic Ocean below. She shuddered. "It would be a long fall from here to the water."

"Don't even think of saying stuff like that," said Carly.

The sisters walked carefully along the edge of the rocky hill, going in the opposite direction from the rock stacks.

Julia noticed a flash of light from the direction of the road. "Carly! There's a vehicle coming up the road. We better hide."

They scrambled behind thick brush and large rocks near where they had hidden their scooters, grateful for adequate cover.

Julia peeked through the brush and watched a black SUV roar into the parking lot. She dared not even breathe, let alone whisper to Carly. Two men she hadn't seen before jumped out of the front seat. One of them carried a small backpack. They picked their way carefully along the rocky ledge for about fifty feet, then disappeared.

Julia and Carly hesitated for only a moment before they quietly followed, hiding behind the dense brush as they moved along the ledge, until they could see the men again.

The two men had dropped down to a lower ledge and were still moving through the brush. They finally stopped next to a huge boulder where the taller of the two tugged on a heavy rope handle and opened a thick, crude wooden door that had been hidden behind heavy vines. He shone a flashlight into an opening and took the backpack from the other man.

"Here'th some food and water," he said with a notable lisp. "You won't be in here muth longer. We're going to take you with us tomorrow when we go to meet the big boat."

Julia heard sobs and a girl's voice.

"Please let me out. There are spiders in here and I'm scared. I promise to behave."

Julia mouthed the word 'Monique' to Carly, who nodded in return.

"It'll be okay," the man said. "I put a blanket in the backpack for you in cathe you're cold in that cave. We'll be back tomorrow about dinner time."

"Hurry up, dude!" The other man spoke with a deep voice. "Boss will get after us if we're late again."

"Yeah, yeah, yeah. I'm coming."

Julia and Carly barely breathed while the men passed within fifteen feet of their hiding place on their return to the parking lot. Julia crept back toward the lot as well, staying hidden. When she heard the engine start, Julia moved quickly to a place where she could see the vehicle as it took off. She memorized the license plate number before it disappeared around the corner, then dictated it into her phone to give to Drew.

Julia and Carly hurried to the door that they'd seen being opened. It would have been impossible to see from the parking lot as it was at least 100 feet away, on a lower ridge, and around a gradual corner. It was invisible unless one knew to look behind the overgrown vines that hung from the ledge above.

The thick, wooden door covering the opening was only eighteen or so inches across and appeared to have been some kind of access door to part of the shaft, perhaps a ventilation access. Julia tugged on the rope but couldn't open the door by herself.

"Let me help you, weakling," Carly said, adding her strength to open the heavy beast of a door. It opened with a loud thud as it hit the rocks alongside the opening.

"Monique?" Julia whispered into the blackness. "Are you Monique?"

She heard broken breathing and soft crying in response.

"I'm Julia and my sister Carly is with me. We've come to get you out of there. Can you move toward me?"

Julia heard scuffling in the darkness, then saw a dark head emerge through the door. Monique crawled out on her hands and knees, dragging the backpack with her. "It's awful in there."

"I'm so glad we found you," said Julia. "The whole island is searching for you."

Julia and Carly helped her to her feet. Monique hugged Julia and Carly tightly for a moment and sobbed. Carly held her close while Julia dug around in the backpack and found the blanket—a pink one, she noticed—and wrapped it around Monique's shoulders. Carly closed the door to the rocky cave. They walked carefully along the rock ledge to where the scooters waited.

"Monique, did they hurt you in any way?" asked Julia.

"No, ma'am."

"We can take you to the doctor if you need to be checked."

Monique shook her head. "They didn't touch me except when they grabbed me and brought me here. I'm sure I'm okay. I just want to go home." She sniffled.

"Of course, you do," said Julia kindly as they approached the scooters. Julia and Carly maneuvered them out from the brush. "Do you think you can hang on to me on the back of this thing and let us get you out of here?"

Monique nodded eagerly.

"Okay." Julia mounted the scooter and Monique got on behind her. "The blanket better go back in the backpack for now."

Monique rolled it up and handed it to Carly, who had taken the backpack from Julia.

"Carly will ride behind us back to town and keep an eye out for bad guys."

Julia heard rustling in the scrub behind her and said, "Shh. I hear something." The three of them stood still, barely breathing. A moment later a small cat emerged from behind the bush.

"It's a kitty!" Monique scrambled off the scooter and swooped it up. "You're too skinny. We need to feed you." She snuggled the cat against her chest, where it promptly started purring loudly.

"How are we going to manage a cat tonight?" asked Julia.

"It's hungry. I heard it crying out here when I was in the cave. Please, can we take it home?"

Julia sighed. "I suppose we can rescue it and find it a good home."

"I think my mom would let me keep it. We don't have a cat right now." Monique got on the back of the scooter, cat and all. "Please?"

"Well, all right. But *you* have to explain it to Rita," said Julia.

"It's kinda pretty, though it is dirty and scrawny," said Carly. "I think it might be a long-haired tortoiseshell. We can tell better in the light at the house. They're almost always female, like calico cats, by the way."

Monique managed a tiny giggle and snuggled the cat. "Thank you. Where are we going? Who's Rita?"

"She and her husband Antonio own the bed-and-breakfast where Carly and I are staying."

Julia asked Carly, "What do you think of going to Rita and Antonio's? Then we can call Drew from there."

"Definitely my first choice."

"Who's Drew?" Monique asked.

"He's the chief of police here," said Julia, looking over her shoulder and smiling sweetly at her passenger. "He'll be very glad to see you."

THE MOON WAS STILL SHINING above the horizon when Julia and Carly entered the house with their precious cargo.

"Oh my," said Rita, jumping up from her chair, where she'd been crocheting.

"Is this Monique?" asked Antonio from his chair in front of his laptop.

"Let me get you something clean to wear," said Rita. "What's with the kitty?"

"Monique will explain in a minute," said Julia.

"I'll warm up some food," said Antonio.

"I'm going to call Drew," said Julia.

THIRTY MINUTES later Drew arrived and met Monique. He hugged her warmly, tears welling up in his eyes. She was able to give him bits and pieces of information that she'd gleaned from conversations amongst the men. The men at the cave called each other "Hank" and "Dude." She thought the one called Hank was the one who played the harmonica because she'd seen one in his hands the day she'd been at the film set. The other guy, Dude, had the lisp from a cleft palate, she reported. The only other name she heard them use was for someone they called "Boss," but she'd not seen him.

Julia and Carly nodded at each other. These guys had to be two of the three they'd overheard at the beach several days before.

Drew asked her more questions about what happened from the time she was finished with the filming and her disappearance.

She told him that she had been walking to the tent to turn in her costume like everyone else. She was the last one, she recalled. She heard someone behind her call her name. When she turned around, she was grabbed from behind and someone stuffed a smelly rag over her mouth. When she woke up, she found herself lying on a blanket in a pitch-black place. Whoever had taken her there had left some snack bars and a couple of bottles of water.

She didn't know what had happened to the costume. She had been carrying it in a small garment bag with the wig and shoes after changing into her regular clothes with the other dancers in the tent that Brock had called the "green room."

When Drew asked why she hadn't answered when the searchers called her name, she said, "It seemed like a long time later when I heard someone calling me but they sounded far away and I couldn't yell loud enough for them to hear me." She started to cry. "I was sure I would never be found when they left." Julia quickly put her arm around Monique's shoulders and held her close.

While she was eager to see her parents, Monique agreed reluctantly to stay with Antonio and Rita for the time being. Rita agreed to keep the cat as long as Monique was there, and found a can of tuna. The cat purred loudly on Monique's lap, as if it also were saying "thank you."

Drew offered to call Monique's parents and tell them she was safe but that her location would be a secret for at least another twenty-four hours. Though her kidnappers had told her they wouldn't be back till the next evening, Drew cautioned her that there was a chance that plans could change and her captors could return sooner and find her gone, and might look for her at her parents' home. "I think it is wiser that they don't know where you are yet, just in case."

He took his leave, with Julia and Carly following him outside.

"I suppose you two think you're going to be in on our rendezvous tomorrow night," he said, grinning.

Julia grinned at him, and Carly flashed her irresistible smile.

"Wouldn't miss it," said Julia.

"I knew that. I'll call Chief Pickett in Road Town in the morning and make plans for how we can intercept these guys. I'm sure he'll go along with you being part of it." He doffed his hat and made a small bow. "You've earned it. Thank you for finding Monique."

Julia inhaled sharply. "I almost forgot about this." She handed him a note with the license plate number. "This might help."

Julia and Carly enjoyed a glass of pinot grigio with their hosts in the tranquil family room. The ceiling fan rotated slowly in the evening air. Rita had turned down the lights and lit a couple of candles. It almost felt like a little celebration. Monique had named the kitty Malla which, she explained, meant Beautiful Singer in some obscure language. She and her new pet were already asleep in the second guest room.

"You two have had quite the day," said Antonio. "What prompted you to go out to the copper mine tonight?"

"Not *my* idea," said Carly. "It was all her," pointing to Julia.

Julia shrugged. "I had this nagging thought that wouldn't go away, and I knew I would be sorry later if I ignored it."

"Maybe you got that from the spirit lady we met at the

beach," said Carly. "She seemed to have some kind of sixth sense too."

Julia raised an eyebrow as she took a sip of her cold wine. "Maybe. I get something like that every now and then. I can't explain it."

Rita raised her glass in a toast to her guests, a glisten of a tear in her eyes. "I like to think it might be my niece Elizabeth helping you. Thank you, my friends, for paying attention to those little whispers, whatever they are."

TWENTY

Friday morning's sunshine seemed a bit brighter with the presence of Monique, who joined Julia and Carly while they enjoyed another of Rita's generous breakfasts.

"I didn't think I would ever see my family and friends again until you two rescued me last night," Monique said quietly. "I wish I could tell them not to worry anymore, but I know the police chief is taking care of talking with them. I get it that he's concerned the word will spread quickly if anyone else knows besides them."

"And that could keep us from capturing the rest of the gang," said Julia. She placed a hand gently on Monique's tiny arm. "And I know you want them put in jail."

"Oh, yes. They are bad men."

"Julia," said Carly, "What if they go to the cave this morning and discover Monique has escaped?"

Monique shook her head. "They wouldn't come in the morning. Too many other people are there because it's a national park. They can come only at night. I don't think they'll miss me today."

"But if you're not there tonight," said Carly, "they'll know something's up."

"The police already know the situation, and I'm sure they have some kind of a stakeout there. But I've got an idea," said Julia. "Maybe they can put a dummy in the cave, just in case. If they *do* go to see her for some reason, they'll hopefully think she's asleep. It would slow them down a little in carrying out their plans, and give the police a little more time to nab them."

"Speaking of plans," she continued, "it's time to leave to meet Drew and find out what he's cooked up for tonight's show." She finished her coffee and picked up the empty breakfast plates. "Monique, you'll stay here with Rita. We can't take the risk that someone might see you and spoil the surprise." She winked at the shy teen.

Monique jumped up and hugged Julia. Julia tenderly brushed her long, dark hair off her pretty face. Carly rose from her chair and put her arms around Monique and her sister.

After another moment, Rita joined the silent trio with a motherly hug.

"Okay, everyone," said Julia. "Let's go meet Drew. Carly and I will be back and clue you in as soon as we can."

Rita stood next to Monique with an arm around her shoulders. "We'll stay out of sight and wait for you here." To her young charge she said, "Perhaps you'll help me bake something."

THE BORROWED scooters knew the way to the police station after making so many trips. Julia and Carly parked their rigs and slipped into the building. Julia had the feeling that everyone knew what they were up to even though no one possibly could. It was the same sense she'd had when she was a teenager—her father always seemed to know what she was going to do before she'd even done it. Her face gave her away, he'd said.

They were ushered into Drew's office. Several uniformed men were there in addition to his fellow officers from the island, whom Julia recalled seeing at the movie set earlier in the week. Drew introduced the new faces as members of the police force from the island of Tortola, which was larger and more populated than Virgin Gorda. He told his audience that he'd talked with the parents of the first girl, Lorena Lejeune, and that she had most likely been killed by the same group that had kidnapped Monique.

Drew continued after introducing Julia and Carly, "We don't have any details of what these guys have planned but these two ladies overheard the two men at the copper mine last night say they would return tonight and that they would take her with them to the 'big boat.'"

"What do you know about their gang?" asked one of the local officers.

Drew arched an eyebrow. "Very little. We believe at least three of them have been on Virgin Gorda this past week. One has a lisp, one has a whiny voice, and one has a very deep voice. One of these jokers plays the harmonica, although we don't know which one that is. A blue and silver harmonica was found on a powerboat at the marina, but we're pretty sure it didn't belong there and was most likely just tossed there. We don't know if it was the same harmonica, of course."

Another of the men asked, "What about the drugs and jewels that were dug up at the beach? Do you know anything more about those?"

Drew raised a finger. "Testing proved that the packets contained cocaine and fentanyl. We have yet to hear back about whether the jewels are authentic, which could mean they are pirate booty. We have no way of knowing when and where they were originally found. If authentic, they could also be jewelry stolen from a private collection and not reported, or from a museum, although that seems less likely. We're operating on the theory that they had been dug up more recently from one of the beaches in the region and are being trafficked along with the illegal drugs. As you know, there are plenty of collectors who don't care whether these items are obtained legally."

Julia dared to raise her hand. "Drew—I mean Chief Hawke —what's going to happen when the kidnappers discover that Monique is no longer in the cave when they go there tonight?"

Drew nodded. "Well, I considered having you or your sister take her place, but I didn't think you'd go for that." He winked as Julia's jaw dropped, then said soberly, "Nor would I want to put you or any other woman in danger. Besides, the fact is that they would know it isn't Monique anyway. Instead, we'll leave it as it is now and assume they'll figure she escaped and will head to their rendezvous without their victim."

"What about arresting these yahoos when they show up tonight at the cave?" asked a third man.

Drew leaned against the wall behind his desk, arms crossed across his chest. "We could do that, but we'd like to get deeper into the organization. I suspect the men we know about here don't have much information that would be useful to capture the leaders. Good question, though. We *will* have someone stationed nearby who will tail our kidnapers after they leave the copper mine. Hopefully, they'll lead us to the big boat, as Monique said they called it."

"What if they panic and don't lead us to the rest of the gang?" asked the first officer.

"We can always arrest them and use other tactics to get

them to talk," said Drew with a wicked grin. He looked around at the men. "Any other questions?"

The men shook their heads and shuffled in their uncomfortable metal chairs.

Drew paced across the front of the small room as he talked. "We obviously don't know what kind of ship they use. It could be one of those pirate ships that sail out of Puerto Rico. It could be a private yacht or sailboat. It could be a big catamaran. They could be using several different rigs. We just don't know, but both the coast guards of both the United Kingdom and the United States have been monitoring some unusual traffic between Miami, San Juan and Venezuela. Almost like when this was part of a major thoroughfare in the 1980s. It died down for a long time but it's getting more difficult for the cartels to travel through Central America and Mexico, I guess." He paused to take a swig of water. "We have a major opportunity tonight to learn more about this nasty organization. We'll have backup air support from San Juan. We also have a couple of private choppers on standby that will be ready to fly on command."

The group of men murmured and nodded to each other.

"The weather will be clear all day and there will be moonlight till after nine tonight. That's probably why they chose this evening to do a rendezvous. We just need to be ready when they act."

He seemed about ready to close the meeting, so once again, Julia raised her hand.

"Were you able to track down that license plate number?" she asked.

Drew shook his head. "It wasn't registered to a specific driver or entity. It's part of a fleet of vans that are rented to a secondary agency. We're still trying to track down someone who can identify that agency. And I'm not optimistic that we'll learn anything today, being as a weekend is coming up. And I hope to have this drug ring in custody before the end of the weekend."

Drew looked across the faces in the room. "Any other questions?" When no one responded, he ended with "That is all."

Julia and Carly waited until the room cleared before approaching Drew. He managed a weak smile and asked, "How can I help you today? Do you have new information?"

"Monique is doing fine so far at the Pacinis' home," said Julia. "Rita invited her to help with some baking when we left the house earlier so she doesn't have so much time to sit around and miss her family."

"That's good."

"And we thought we'd go to Sonja's house next and ask about the guys hanging out at the movie set that might have been the ones who kidnapped Monique. We were going to go last evening but got sidetracked. Is that still okay with you, considering that we've now found Monique?"

Drew nodded. "Anything you can find out about them will be a bonus. I still hope to identify any local connections that are involved with this gang. But do be careful."

"Of course. Maybe Sonja will tell us something to help you break the case. Carly and I want to do this for Lorena and Monique." *And Elizabeth*, she thought to herself.

TWENTY-ONE

J ulia called Rita to see if things were going okay. She had a niggling worry that Monique might be sneakier than they thought and try to reach her parents. She was relieved to hear that so far things were going well and that Monique had a knack for baking. "We'll be back in a couple of hours," said Julia, ending the call.

Turning to Carly she said, "Let's head out to Sonja's and see what she has to say."

"Now would be a good time, probably," said Carly. "Do you have an address for her?"

"No, but Sally Ritchie, the dance studio owner, probably does and I already have her phone number."

"She might even be at the studio for Saturday classes," said Carly. "It's only a few blocks away. Let's go there first."

The studio was abuzz with young dancers, but Sonja's group wasn't among them. Ms. Ritchie was happy to share the address she had on file and confirmed the phone number.

"Sonja's had a rough life, so I hope you'll be kind with her," said Sally. "She was orphaned as a youngster and has been in foster care as long as I've taught her. I think this is the third or fourth family that she's lived with." She shook her head with a sad smile on her face.

"That's hard on a kid," said Julia. "So were there no grandparents or other relatives who could have taken her in?"

"Apparently not. Either there wasn't anyone available, or they weren't able to provide for her." Sally sighed. "It seems like she's always trying to fit in somewhere. She seems happiest when she's here dancing. And she's quite good."

"It sounds like she's lucky to have you in her corner," said Julia.

Sally beamed. "Thank you. She's almost like a daughter to me."

THE ADDRESS for Sonja's foster family was about a mile north of town proper. Julia and Carly followed North Sound Road until they found where it branched into two main roads. They turned onto Nail Bay Road, which went left toward the Caribbean Sea, and drove another half mile or so to a small road labeled Allegro that seemed more like a driveway.

"These are really nice homes out here," said Carly when they paused to check final instructions. "I wouldn't mind living this close to the beach."

"They don't look like the kind of homes I expected for a foster family," said Julia. "Certainly not what I recall from our hometown growing up."

"Stereotyping, huh?" teased Carly.

"Sally's note says it's the last house on the road." Julia turned to Carly. "Are you ready?"

Carly nodded and throttled her scooter.

The house itself was on the small side, compared to others

they'd passed on the way. It looked clean, was painted white, had a red roof like many of the neighbors, and sported a partially covered deck that ran across the front of the upper level.

Julia and Carly looked at each other and walked up to what they assumed was a front door. They knocked and waited. They heard a woman yelling to someone to answer the door, and a dog barking. A dark-haired boy who appeared to be about five or six years old pulled the door open. He smiled a toothy grin that was missing a front upper tooth.

"Who are you?" he asked. "Are you here for Sonja?" He turned and yelled, "Mom, it's two ladies." He left the door open and bounced across the small room where he joined two other children, one older and one younger, who were playing a video game of some kind.

A nicely dressed woman emerged from a back room. She came to a stop when she noticed Julia and Carly standing at the door. "Oh. I thought you would be from the agency. How can I help you?"

Julia offered a hand, as did Carly. "Hi. I'm Julia, and this is my sister Carly. We met Sonja a couple of days ago at the dance studio and have a couple of questions for her."

The woman's face paled. "Why would you be asking her questions? Has she done something?"

Julia smiled. "No, nothing like that. We hoped she could tell us what happened the day Monique disappeared."

"Oh. That." She stepped aside and said, "Come on into the kitchen. It's quieter there."

They stepped cautiously around the toys scattered across the small room and followed her into a compact, brightly lit kitchen with yellow walls and blue accents.

"I was just making tea. Would you care for some?"

Her guests nodded. She plucked three cups from a

cupboard and plopped teabags into them. The tea kettle was already steaming and ready to pour. She set a small pitcher of milk and a sugar bowl on the table and joined them there.

"I'm Teresa Reynolds," she said as she added milk to her tea. "Sonja's my foster daughter. She's been with us for three years." She tasted her drink and added some sugar. "She's never given us any trouble. Is there something I don't know about?"

Julia shook her head. "No, we're not aware of anything like that. Is she home?"

"Not at the moment. She left a while ago with the guy she's been seeing. She said she'd be back after lunch. Why? What's going on?"

Julia took a big breath. "We can't be sure, but when Carly and I talked to her at dance class we got the sense that she knew more than she was telling about Monique's disappearance."

"Well, Sonja was very upset about what happened and told me she was worried that it might have been her fault."

"Sonja's fault?" asked Julia.

"Why would she think so?" asked Carly.

"I'm not sure, but I got the impression that Sonja had something to do with connecting the dance studio with the director of the movie that's being filmed on the island. You know, because they wanted dancers."

"How did she know about that?" Julia asked, recalling a statement that local kids had been hanging out on the set during the filming.

Mrs. Reynolds laughed nervously. "You know how teenagers are. They all want to be movie stars at this age. A bunch of them have been going to the beach after school and watching the film crew and actors as they do the shooting. I guess they hope they'll get to be extras or something." She shrugged. "It seemed like a harmless activity and better than them getting tattoos and vaping."

Julia nodded. "I'm sure it's the most exciting thing going on around here right now. I'd probably be doing the same thing if I were that age." Julia didn't add that both she and Carly had briefly had it in their minds when they first heard about the filming that they, too, might be extras.

"They filmed some of the scenes for the *Twilight* movie at our old high school," said Carly. "One of my friends played a volleyball coach, but he only got about two seconds in the final version. I had to watch really closely or I would have missed him."

"Well, he's still got bragging rights," said Julia. She sipped on the tea, holding her hands around the warm cup. She turned to Teresa and asked, "What is the name of this guy she's seeing today?"

"She hasn't told me yet and it's almost like she's afraid if she gives him a name, he won't be real. Like a figment of her imagination. I haven't pushed her about it because most of her boyfriends don't last long."

"Hm," said Julia. She finished her tea. "Okay, Mrs. Reynolds, I hope you'll have Sonja call when she gets home." Julia handed her a business card. "She can call anytime."

"I'll do that. And please call me Teresa. 'Mrs. Reynolds' sounds like my mother-in-law."

WALKING BACK TO THE SCOOTERS, Julia said, "Do you suppose we should find Noah and see if he can tell us more about the local admiring teens? Maybe he heard something when they were filming."

"Sure," said Carly. "We can show him the photos we have

of Sonja and see what he remembers of her when she was on the set. You do have a photo, don't you?"

"Yes. I took a couple when we were watching them dance at the studio before we interviewed them." Julia pulled out her cell and opened the photo gallery. "Hm. Where'd they go?" She frowned and scrolled the other direction. "Okay. Here's a good one of Sonja with two other girls, although I don't know which is which, and another that shows both Sonja and Annalee." She showed them to Carly.

"I've got Noah's number," said Carly. "Shall I call him now?"

"Sure. It's Saturday, so maybe he's free. See if he'll meet us at the Sapphire."

CHAPTER
TWENTY-TWO

The late Friday-morning crowd at the Sapphire was skewed toward men who were still there after having Bloody Marys with their breakfast—or maybe the drinks *had* been their breakfast, Julia thought to herself. Julia and Carly scanned the clientele for Noah. Carly saw him first, standing at the bar leaning and on an elbow. He seemed to be watching them look for him. He winked at her when she waved at him and pointed toward a corner table.

"What took you so long?" Noah spun a chair around and settled his long legs on either side. "I expected you to call me a long time ago."

"Huh?" Julia arched an eyebrow. "Why would we be calling you?"

He laughed. "I'm just teasing. You ladies don't seem like the type to fall for us movie stars."

"Well, we did have some questions." Carly noticed he didn't have a drink. "Sorry if you've been waiting long. Did you have a drink already?"

"Not yet. I just got here but I ordered a beer. I sure need one."

He sighed. "I'm just stressed over this movie bit. Stubby—Brock—wants to finish the filming by next week but the work has been interrupted by the investigation into that girl's disappearance. And now there are questions about the security company."

"What does that have to do with the filming schedule?" asked Julia.

"It means we can't do anything until the police are done asking questions." He paused to accept the beer he had ordered at the bar and waited while Julia and Carly placed orders for themselves. "I'll get those," he said to the waitress.

"I thought the police were all done with that," said Carly. "What other scenes do you still have to film anyway?"

Noah scoffed. "They're not going to be done until they find the girl—"

"Her name is Monique," Julia reminded him.

"Or her body," he finished.

Julia and Carly looked at each other from either side of Noah. Julia gently shook her head. "I know you said you hadn't noticed anything the day the dance students were there but sometimes people recall details later. What about you? Is there any tidbit, even if it seems minor, that might be helpful?"

Noah looked off toward the turquoise blue water where the sunlight danced off the gentle waves. "I'm not sure if this is anything, but one of the guys wearing a security uniform looked really young, like he was barely a teenager. And he wasn't one of the men we saw all the other days."

"Any other details? Height? Hair color? General description?"

"He was maybe five foot ten and skinny. I thought his pants might fall off, but he had a belt cinched tight. He had dark, curly hair that needed a cut."

"Go on."

"And he had a lisp when he talked. But most of the time he just stood there and didn't say anything."

Julia waited to respond until the waitress served the wine she and Carly had ordered. "Thank you," she said to the waitress.

"Did you tell the police about the lisp?" asked Julia, sensing Carly's eyes staring at her.

"They didn't ask me about him. I figured they'd talk to the security company."

"Was he one of their regulars?"

"I don't know, but I only saw him that one day. Do you think that's important?"

"I'm going to call Chief Hawke and you can tell him what you just told me, and anything else that comes to mind."

Julia was able to reach the police chief directly. She gave him a brief heads up and handed the phone to Noah. She and Carly sipped on their drinks while Noah related his story, and then answered a few questions with answers of "yes" and "no."

"Yes, sir, I will ... Of course ... Goodbye." Noah ended the call and handed Julia her phone. "I don't think he likes me very much."

Julia smiled kindly. "He's frustrated over the situation like everyone else is. His job is to keep the people of the island safe and right now he's feeling some heat. As I'm sure you can understand."

"Yeah, I do. I hope he finds Monique. I really do."

Julia picked up her phone and opened the photo gallery. "I took these photos at the dance studio. Do you recognize the taller girl? Her name is Sonja."

Noah peered at the two pictures. "I think both of those girls were in the dancing gig. The one you call Sonja has been around the set several other times, though. She seemed to know one of the security guys."

"The one who lisped?" asked Julia.

"No. That guy only came once, that I saw. It was one of the regulars who came almost every day." He finished his beer. "Gotta run. I have some lines to practice just in case we get to do more filming next week." He did a quasi-salute with his empty glass and sauntered toward the bar, where he left the glass and said a few words to the cute waitress, who promptly blushed.

Carly shook her head. "He's an impossible flirt, but he sure is adorable."

"You have to remind yourself that he *is* an actor," said Julia. "I'm not sure I can tell what's real and what's a put-on with him." She finished her wine and left a tip for the waitress. "Let's go back to the house and see how Monique is doing. We can tell her about Sonja at the same time."

A DELICIOUS AROMA of vanilla mingled with coconut wafted into their noses when Julia and Carly opened the door. Monique proudly held up a tray of freshly crafted cookies, still warm from the oven. The smile on her face was a welcome sight.

Rita had been ready to serve tea and added two cups and saucers to the table. "I think I've found an assistant for my bakery business." She grinned at Monique and gave her a one-arm hug.

"A bakery business? Are you serious?" Julia took a couple of cookies for herself and handed two more to Carly.

Rita poured the brewed tea and nodded. "I've been thinking about it for a while now. Antonio is so busy with his own business, and I find myself with lots of time on my hands.

I thought a small bakery would be a perfect complement to the bed-and-breakfast."

"What a smart idea," said Julia.

"You certainly know how to bake," said Carly, licking crumbs off her fingers.

"Monique could help me with the baking, as well as deliveries. There's a small boutique shop downtown that would be willing to sell whatever I make."

"I could make home deliveries, too," said Monique. "I know where everything is on the island."

Rita smiled broadly at her young helper. "That's another good idea."

"We went to Sonja's house this morning and talked with her foster mom, Teresa Reynolds," said Julia. "Sonja wasn't home." She looked at Monique, whose smile disappeared.

"Monique, do you know who she's been seeing lately? Her mom mentioned she was with a guy today."

"He's not from here," Monique replied quietly. "I heard Sonja say he's been coming over from Tortola."

"Do you know a name, by any chance?" Julia nibbled on her cookies. "Yum, delicious. Good job, Monique."

Monique blushed. "I haven't heard her say a name. I only know about him from seeing her with him after dance class a couple of times. Sonja's ahead of me in school and doesn't share stuff like that with us younger girls," she said with a scoff.

"Have you seen him anywhere else around town?" asked Julia.

"No, except I think I saw him the day we danced at the movie set. He was standing in the shade by the tents where we all turned in our costumes and wigs. I didn't see him when I came out." Monique stiffened with a sudden realization. "Do you think he had something to do with kidnapping me?"

CHAPTER

TWENTY-THREE

"We haven't heard from Sonja yet," said Julia to Carly after lunch.

"Mrs. Reynolds didn't give us an exact time that she would be home."

"I know. I just thought she'd call sooner than this."

"You can worry about that if you want to," said Carly. "I'm going to get another cookie or two and check on Monique. She's supposed to be working on the homework that her mom sent over for her."

"That was really nice of Drew to get her assignments. At least it gives her something to do."

Carly padded to the kitchen for cookies for herself and Monique. She peeked into the guest room where Monique was sitting cross-legged on the bed with a book perched on a knee and a notebook lying on the bedcovers.

"Hey," said Carly. "How're you doing?" She handed her the cookies and a glass of milk.

"I'm kinda bored, but this is tons better than being in that cave." She shuddered and said, "Ugh. There were icky things in there. And it was terrible to be in total blackness."

Carly sat on the edge of the bed. "I know what you mean. I was kidnapped by art smugglers in Amsterdam a while back. They blindfolded me and had me tied up. I was terrified that Julia wouldn't find me in time. But she came through. So far she's got a perfect record for rescues."

"What about her record for finding out who killed that little girl that you found on the beach?"

"How do you know about that?"

Monique shrugged. "We hear things at school. Someone said she was dressed like we were in the pirate movie." She looked up at Carly. "Is that true?"

Carly nodded.

"Do you think I might have ended up dead, too? If you hadn't found me?"

Carly pressed her lips together. "Possibly. But we found you in time."

"But you and Julia think that the same people who killed her kidnapped me and that's why I can't go home yet. Right?"

"Yes, that's right. We're very glad we found you before anything worse happened."

Monique sighed and reached up to hug Carly. "Me, too." Her eyes welled up with tears. "I hope Chief Hawke and the policemen catch the bad guys soon. I want to go home."

They both jumped when they heard a loud rap on the door followed by Julia's entrance. Her face was pale.

"Bad news," said Julia. "Mrs. Reynolds, Sonja's foster mom, just called. Sonja isn't home yet and isn't answering her phone. She was supposed to be home by one o'clock to take the boys to a swimming lesson. Teresa—Mrs. Reynolds—is worried. She said this is totally out of character for Sonja. She's usually very reliable."

"Are we going to look for her?" asked Carly. "Where would we even start?"

"I've already called Drew and he'll mobilize the neighborhood teams for an island search."

"Maybe she'll show up and it'll turn out to be a big false alarm," said Carly.

"We can only hope. And, of course, Monique will be safe as long as she's with Rita." Julia glanced at Monique who was vigorously nodding, her eyes big. Julia walked across the room and enveloped the scared teen in a comforting hug. "You've helped us with what you told us about the guys who came to the cave. That makes it easier to find Sonja, if she doesn't show up on her own." Julia kissed her gently on the forehead.

Monique followed Julia and Carly into the family room. "I want to go with you when you go," she said, "but I know I can't. But promise me you'll call and let me know when you find Sonja."

"Yes, we will." Julia turned to Carly. "Drew said we could check the cave at the copper mine. One of his officers will be waiting there for us at the top of the hour."

THE PARKING LOT at the Copper Mine National Park was half-full at the early afternoon hour. Julia and Carly rode in opposite directions through the area looking for a black SUV, but saw none. They parked near the uniformed policeman, who stood guard at the ledge of the cliff fifty or so feet from the door to Monique's former prison. Officer Monte Manudo was keeping the park visitors away from the cliff where the cave was hidden around the corner, out of direct view.

Once the officer gave them the go-ahead, Julia and Carly scrambled over the rocks, then walked carefully along the ledge to the cave where they tugged on the rope handle. The shallow shaft was empty of humans. Julia was disappointed; she had hoped that Sonja would be there, as Monique had been.

Carly and Julia walked back to the parking lot, faces grim.

"No Sonja," Julia announced.

TWENTY-FOUR

J ulia and Carly motored back into town. Julia's thoughts were on the events coming up later. Drew had told her earlier that he would call her back as soon as he knew the overall plan for the evening. She didn't like waiting for the unknown. She liked having a map and a schedule to guide her, even on vacation. As they neared the bed-and-breakfast, she pulled off the road and waited for Carly to stop as well.

"Why are you stopping here?"

"I was just thinking of one of the comments that one of the mystery guys made when we were eavesdropping on the beach a few days ago," said Julia. "They mentioned that they were going to go to Mountain Trunk Bay."

"And you want to go there now, I suppose."

"What if we find something there that will help us find Sonja or that will lead us to this gang?"

Carly harrumphed. "What if we show up there and they have guns? I say we call Drew instead and let his men go there."

"If they *are* there, they won't know who we are. We'll just be tourists looking for a nice beach."

"They might know our faces if they've been at the film set when we were there."

"But we haven't asked any of them direct questions, so why would they think we're anyone other than friends of Noah?"

Carly groaned and rolled her eyes. "Okay. Let's go but only long enough to see if there's a nice beach where we should have gone snorkeling. I'll follow you."

"It's not far from Savannah Bay, past the turnoff to Sonja's house. Ten or twelve minutes away at the most."

JULIA HAD her doubts about finding the beach once they passed the village at Mahoe Bay. The road didn't seem to get close enough to a beach to be the one they were looking for. After another several minutes, she saw a few houses and increasing evidence of civilization; then she spotted a sign that directed them to beach access at Mountain Trunk Bay. They parked the scooters at a trailhead and scampered down the path to the beach.

"The water here is beautiful," said Carly. "Should have brought the snorkel gear."

"Yes, it is. I wonder what was so interesting about this beach. I doubt they were looking for a place to snorkel." She snickered. "There are a lot of houses nearby. And I don't see a marina where a boat could be moored, if that's the reason they were supposed to check it out."

"Sometimes when we go up the Lewis River we pull our powerboat up on the beach for a while and have a picnic," said Carly. "You don't have to have a marina to park a boat."

They walked along the beach as far as they could until they ran into a rocky ledge with no definable trail along the shore. Julia took some photos for future reference and said, "I say we go back to the scooters and drive around to the other side of this point. Maybe there's something more interesting there."

"I agree," said Carly.

A short distance up the road they found another place to park with a path to the beach. The beautiful sand stretched out for several hundred yards from the rocky point behind them to another one ahead.

"Nice beach," said Carly. "I bet they don't get much tourist traffic out here."

"But still no marinas for a boat launch. And no boats pulled up on the beach."

"Maybe they used the beach for buried treasure," said Carly.

"It's as good a thought as any. I'll take a few photos and then we should head back."

"Wait a sec. I see a huge boat approaching the corner from the left. It seems really close to shore."

"I see it. I think that would qualify as a yacht. It must be at least fifty feet long. I wonder why it's going so slowly," said Julia.

"There's a small powerboat coming from the right. It looks like it's heading to the yacht. Take some pictures, Julia."

"Roger, that. I'll take a video. Maybe this will make sense to Drew when he sees it later."

Julia and Carly watched as the powerboat approached the yacht and slowed down when it got closer. When it was within ten feet or so someone on the yacht tossed a line to a person in the smaller boat. He tied off, then reached up to accept a satchel of some kind from someone on the yacht reaching over the rail. A second satchel followed, then the smaller boat untied the line and sped off from whence it came and disappeared around the point.

"Drat," said Julia. "I can't see where it went from here. There are too many houses and trees blocking my view around the corner."

"The yacht is heading off the other direction and is moving away from the island," said Carly. "It looks like it's speeding up."

"Let's take the scooters up the road a little farther," said Julia. "Maybe there's a marina or dock that the powerboat is using."

"It's getting late. How about checking for a marina or dock on the map on your phone instead? You can look at the satellite view when we get back to the house."

"Good idea, sis. I'll send this to Drew. He would know if there were a marina or docking space around here. I wonder if those satchels contained drugs. Do you remember reading about some guys doing something like this along the Columbia River? It was a long time ago, though."

"I'm sure I was just a child." Carly laughed and sped off, with Julia close behind.

THEY WERE HALFWAY home when Julia pulled to the side of the road. Carly joined her.

"Why are we stopping this time?" Carly asked. She looked around. "This looks like where we stopped that first day and found Lorena."

"I have this inkling that won't go away about the spirit woman, Amaya. What if she knows something else but doesn't know how to find us?" Julia hopped off her scooter and started walking down the trail toward the beach.

"Where are you going?" Carly asked as she caught up with her sister.

"I think if we go into the forest from the rock where we met Amaya, we'll find her. I just know, and I can't tell you how I know, that she's waiting for us."

Carly scrunched up her face and said, "Brother. Like that's going to help us find her."

The sisters silently followed a sandy trail through the tropical flora. It soon became harder to follow and then the faint trail disappeared completely.

"I hope you left breadcrumbs for us to find our way back, Girl Scout," said Carly.

Julia stood and looked in all directions for a sign like a broken tree limb that she could use to follow a trail to Amaya, thinking she must live somewhere in the forest. "I don't see anything, but I hear soft voices coming from somewhere up ahead."

Carly strained to listen. "I hear something too. It sounds like chanting. And I hear drums beating."

Julia and Carly headed in the direction of the sounds, moving stealthily. Julia didn't want to run into a tribe that practiced head-shrinking, although her logical self poohpoohed the thought. Carly held onto her hand as they moved slowly toward the chants, which grew louder as they went farther into the forest of trees and shrubs.

They stopped behind a mature palm tree when they saw a clearing ahead where a dozen or so people seemed to be dancing around a small urn. They moved slowly in a counterclockwise circle. Suddenly the drum beats thundered and all the dancers stopped. An older man wearing a short sarong stepped into the center of the circle. He bowed toward the urn, said a few words, then picked it up and handed it to a woman. She accepted it with a bow and held it to her chest. The circle moved around the woman and the urn one more time. The dancers then disappeared into the forest. It was as if they had never been there.

Julia felt a gentle tap on her left shoulder. She stifled a scream as she jumped. She knew Carly was still standing next to her on the right because she still clung onto her hand. She tugged on Carly's hand and made a head movement to her left. They both turned to see Amaya smiling at them. Julia exhaled, not realizing she had been holding her breath.

"Amaya! How did you know we were here?" Julia asked.

Amaya bowed her head and said, "My spirit told me that you were coming and that I would find you here."

Julia's skin prickled. She'd had strange sensations of her own at times that she couldn't explain in any logical way. Now she wondered if a spirit had been trying to get her attention.

"We're glad to see you," said Julia. "What was that dance we were watching?"

"Our people sent the spirit of the woman's husband to his afterlife. She can sleep peacefully now that he has gone to where she cannot yet go."

"I thought it seemed like a ceremony of some kind," said Julia. "A funeral makes sense."

"Why are you looking for me? Did you know I have something for you?"

Julia shook her head. "I ... I ... I just had this thought that you had something to tell us. I can't explain any better than that."

"I thought she was acting crazy," said Carly.

Amaya smiled and said, "Follow me."

The sisters followed the spirit woman through the maze of tropical trees and plants. The path seemed circuitous. Julia wondered if that was to make it difficult for others to track her. Eventually they came to a crude hut made of bamboo with a thatched roof of palm leaves. Amaya invited them into the cozy space and pointed to two cushions on the floor. She went through a curtain into a second room, saying, "Wait. I have something to show you."

Julia and Carly sat like little girls waiting for a movie to start, excited and wondering what that "something" would be. The room in which they waited was more round than square.

Julia noticed the crude carvings which adorned the walls all around them and wondered if they had special meaning, knowing that Amaya was a descendant of a shaman. Amaya stepped into the room a couple of minutes later carrying a cinnamon-colored leather bag.

"I found this in the sand yesterday. I watched two men bury it near a rock and waited till dark to get it." She took out a piece of jewelry and handed it to Julia. She said, "This is one of the bracelets I found in the bag—the prettiest one. I hope it will help you find the bad man who killed the Lejeune girl."

Julia and Carly admired the beautiful bracelet. It was gold with purple and turquoise stones. It had a crude clasp and appeared to be very old.

"This is lovely, Amaya," said Julia. "Can you describe the men? Could you tell if they were locals?"

Amaya shook her head. "They were dressed in black and were too far away for me to see what they looked like. One of them played a funny-sounding instrument. I have not heard one before. It sounded like a sick seagull crying. It hurt my ears." She covered her ears and shook her head, looking skyward.

"We've heard someone play a harmonica that sounded just like that. It might be the same instrument," said Carly, laughing with Julia.

"That is all I know." Amaya took the bracelet and put it in

the small sack with the others. "Will you take these to the police?"

"Of course," said Julia. "Maybe this will be the break we need to find the murderer. Thank you."

"Can you tell us how to get back to the road?" asked Carly. "I don't trust Julia's sense of direction."

"Come with me. I will lead you to the rock where we first met."

The trio walked silently through the trees. Amaya stopped when they were in sight of the rock at the edge of the forest. "Goodbye, my friends. Follow the truth." To Julia, she added, "Learn to trust your spirit."

ALL WAS quiet at the bed-and-breakfast when Julia and Carly popped into the house. Rita was sitting at her computer looking for recipes for her bakery, she told them. Antonio had gone to meet a friend at his yacht to talk business. Monique was listening to music in her room.

Julia sent a quick message to Drew with a photo of the jewelry from Amaya that was now in her possession. She also sent the video of the yacht and potential drug exchange.

Drew called back immediately to ask for additional details and to give them the plan for the evening.

"We're counting on the kidnappers waiting till early evening to go to the copper mine because tourists frequently go there in the afternoon. No sense in calling attention to their secret cave in case someone is hanging around," he said.

"And to avoid the possibility of Monique screaming her head off, if she were to still be there." Julia chuckled. "I would love to be the chipmunk at the scene when they open the door and she's not there."

"She's still safe with you at Antonio and Rita's, isn't she?" Drew said, a touch of panic in his voice.

"Yes. I hope she understands the potential danger to her or her parents if anyone besides us knows where she is."

"Good. I'm going to send Lenny, my second-in-command, to collect you and your sister at around seven thirty. We're working with other agencies to coordinate air surveillance and coast guard presence for when we catch up with these guys."

"Okay. This takes me back to when *I* was the one being rescued several years ago in St. Maarten."

"I'm not sure I know that story."

"Oh, it's not a big deal," said Julia. "I'll tell you later."

Julia updated Carly, Rita and Monique—who had emerged from her room when she heard her name in the conversation—of the plan for the evening. "Drew didn't give me any more detail than that. I'm probably not at the 'need to know' level for the big stuff." She smiled and gave Monique a little hug.

Monique asked, "Am I allowed to go with you?" She looked hopefully at Julia, then Rita.

Julia and Rita looked at each other with furrowed brows, then Rita said, "Honey, I know you would love to be part of catching these guys, but I don't think we should put you in any potential danger since we're not your parents."

Julia said, "We'd have to clear that idea with—"

The unexpected sound of the back door opening and closing interrupted Julia's response. Antonio bounded into the living room, then stopped when he noticed the four sets of eyes staring at him. "Did I interrupt something?"

Julia explained Drew's plan and Monique's request. Antonio nodded slowly before saying, "I have a better idea for you, Mademoiselle Monique."

"What is it?" she asked eagerly.

"I told Julia and Carly a few days ago that I have some

connections with my former buddies in communications from when I worked for the government." He looked at Julia. "We think we have a bead on a mega yacht that's been working the waters between Puerto Rico and Venezuela."

"Did Drew tell you we saw a yacht making a rendezvous with a powerboat near Mountain Trunk Bay earlier?" Julia asked, eyes wide. She pulled up the video and shared it with Antonio.

He jotted down a couple of notes. "I'll share this with the others. It may well be another piece of the puzzle."

Monique asked, "What is your better idea for me, Monsieur Antonio?"

Antonio grinned as though he'd just eaten something delicious from the morning's baking session. "How would you like to help me while I monitor the rendezvous from right here? Several of us will be on our computers keeping track of what's going on. You would be safe and involved at the same time."

"I'd like that," said Monique.

Julia asked with narrowed eyes, "What kind of job did you have in your former life?"

Antonio arched an eyebrow. "Top secret." Then he winked.

TWENTY-FIVE

J ulia's skin prickled with anticipation as seven thirty neared. She could sense Carly's nervousness. Her sister was drying dishes for Rita with great fervor. And she was quieter than usual.

Everyone in the house jumped when the doorbell chimed. Drew himself stood at the door when Rita opened it.

"It's time to go after these guys," he said. "Are you ready, Julia and Carly?"

"We were expecting Lenny, but you'll do," Julia said as Carly nodded eagerly. "Before I forget, let me give you the jewels we got from Amaya, the spirit woman." She retrieved the bag of precious gems from its hiding place in an empty flour canister in Rita's pantry.

Drew whistled. "I'm sure these are worth a pretty penny." He turned to Rita. "Why don't you keep these until I ask for them later? They're probably safer here than in my police car for the moment." He handed the rustic bag to her and nodded his thanks.

"Let's head out, ladies," he said, opening the door.

Julia and Carly each hugged Monique, who huddled close to Rita. Rita kissed them both on the cheek as they left, and Antonio followed them out the door.

"Are you going with us?" Julia asked Antonio.

"No, but I want to assure you you're in good hands. I trust Drew and his team with your lives. I can tell you more later." He saluted the sisters as they climbed into the official SUV with Drew at the wheel. Antonio waved and stood with hands on his hips as the vehicle drove away.

"Earlier you said you were sending your second-in-command to get us," said Julia.

"Yeah. We had to modify our plans. I sent him off in a chopper."

They had driven only a short distance when Julia's phone lit up with a message. She read aloud, "'Teresa here. Sonja called. She said she's okay for now but scared and can't tell me anything more. She said to hurry before they take her away.'" Julia, in the front passenger's seat, looked at Drew. "I think I should call Teresa. She's Sonja's foster mom. Maybe she can tell me a little more."

"Go ahead," said Drew. "Ask her if she has a number for the phone her daughter called from."

Julia quickly made the call. Mrs. Reynolds' voice trembled over the phone. "It was her own phone. She said she'd hid it and was calling from the bathroom at the place where she was being held. That was all she had time for. I could tell Sonja had been crying."

"Did you hear anything in the background? Like some kind of noise that could give you a location? You know: boat horns, or that sort of thing."

"Nothing like that, but someone was playing a harmonica. Badly, I might add."

Julia's heart sped up. She dared a look at Carly, whose eyes were open wide.

"Okay, Teresa. Thank you. Carly and I are with Chief Hawke right now. Say your prayers and keep your fingers crossed. We hope to find Sonja and bring her home. Bye."

Drew grunted. "That harmonica keeps showing up. Damn! Let's hope we have some luck with us tonight."

Sonja had finally quit struggling in an attempt to loosen the ropes that held her tight in the uncomfortable chair. At least she wasn't blindfolded anymore. That had been horrible.

"You said you were going to let me go after I told you about the spirit lady," Sonja had said after the man with the lisp secured her hands to the back of the chair.

"That was before I found your phone. Now I can't let you go."

"You promised!" Sonja exclaimed.

The shorter man laughed. "I lied. And why would we do that? We have plans for you. Boss man said to keep you after all."

"Who's 'boss man'?"

"Now, now, little girl," said the second man, the one who lisped. "You'll meet him when we go to the big boat."

"I have to pee. Bad."

The shorter man groaned. "Again? You just peed a half hour ago. You'll have to wait a few minutes while I take care of some things."

"What things?"

"You talk too much. Be quiet or I won't take you to the bathroom."

"Then you'll have to clean up a mess."

"No, I'll make you clean it up."

Sonja smirked. "But then you'd have to untie my hands."

DREW HAD STATIONED two of the officers at the Copper Mine in anticipation of someone arriving to retrieve Monique from her cave prison. Shortly after eight p.m., Jack, one of the officers borrowed from the Road Town police, called with the news that a black SUV had shown up with two men inside. They had been surprised and audibly angry to find the cave empty.

Jack told Drew, "I heard some words I'm sure I've never heard before." He chuckled. "One of them said something about what the boss man would do when they arrived without the girl. We're following them from a distance now. They're headed north on North Sound Road."

"Roger. There are a couple of small docks up on that end of the island. They may have a powerboat waiting. That's not far from where Julia and her sister saw the rendezvous with the yacht earlier."

"We'll let you know if they turn off anywhere."

"We're headed out on the police patrol boat. Our eyes in the sky are tracking what we think is the mother ship. It's currently on the north side of Puerto Rico, headed east."

"Yes, sir. We'll await further instructions."

Drew had distributed weather gear and life vests to the girls. Julia had wondered why they needed the waterproof jacket and overalls but now that the twenty-eight-foot TP Marine RIB patrol boat was moving at a fast clip through the choppy water, she was grateful.

"Where are we going?" Julia asked. "I hope we're not going to try to rendezvous with the yacht you mentioned."

Drew turned and smiled at her. "No, we'll leave that to the

Coast Guard. Their rigs are much bigger and faster and capable of intercepting bigger boats than we can with our patrol boats."

"So where are we going?" Carly asked.

"There's a thirty-two-foot Parker patrol boat waiting for us in Road Town. It has twin 300-horsepower outboard motors and is much faster and more powerful than this one. It's also more comfortable. The U.S. Coast Guard has sent its eighty-five-foot patrol boat, USCGC *Reef Shark*, from San Juan. Its plan is to approach the main yacht once we have reasonable evidence that a drug transfer is in process. The video you sent me helped identify one of the accessory yachts that we suspect is part of a much bigger ring."

"I didn't realize the Coast Guard covered this area," said Julia.

"Puerto Rico and the United States Virgin Islands are part of the territory protected by the U.S. Coast Guard. The British Virgin Islands are protected by the United Kingdom Coast Guard through VISAR, our Virgin Islands Search and Rescue system, but we have an agreement between the countries that allows us to cooperate in situations like this."

"Wow," said Carly. "I can hardly wait to tell my hubby about *this* trip."

SONJA LISTENED to the conversation that the shorter man—Hank, she thought was his name—was having with someone on his cell as he entered her prison again.

"Yes, Boss. We have the girl here. She's pretty feisty but we have her tied up good." He glared at Sonja. She made a face at him in return and stomped her feet.

"We'll be at the boat in about twenty minutes. Is Luke

meeting us there?" He gestured to his partner to listen in on the phone.

After a minute or so of listening to what must have been some kind of instructions, he replied, "Okay, Boss. We'll leave right now."

Sonja stopped wiggling. *Was Luke part of this gang? Why had she trusted him? Or was he going to rescue her?* A part of her panicked. She'd heard the stories about the girl who was found on the beach earlier in the week, and that she'd been dressed in the same kind of kimono that the dancers had worn for the movie. Her heart fell with a thud and tears welled up in her eyes. A moment later she screamed when Hank came up behind her and clapped a smelly rag over her face.

NOAH TURNED in his costume and removed his makeup after the filming for the day. Brock had kept them shooting the same scene again and again. He wanted to catch the best lighting, he'd said. Noah was a bit miffed because Luke had been released for the day at the end of the morning and had left Noah without his expected ride back to their rented rooms. At least he had the weekend off, he mused as he approached one of the security guards for a ride. Maybe he would run into Julia and Carly again. They were fun to visit with and he enjoyed chatting and flirting with them, especially the blonde sister Carly. He pulled out his cell to call.

TWENTY-SIX

The black SUV continued driving north, trailed by the unmarked police car with Jack at the wheel, Ray Townsend riding shotgun.

"This guy is in a big hurry," said Jack. "He must have a hot date." He chuckled and checked the vehicle's GPS screen. "There's a marina up ahead according to the map. I wonder if that's where he's headed."

"Maybe, but right now he's turning off onto a side road up ahead," said Ray. "I can just see a light through the trees on the right. You'd better slow down. I think we should wait and see what they do next." He looked at the detailed island map in his hands. "There's no other posted outlet for that road so they'll have to come back out the same way, I would think."

"I'll let Drew know so he can send a chopper this way if we need backup," said Jack. "Let's give them ten minutes before we do anything."

❧

Noah checked his phone contact list but much to his chagrin, he didn't have a number entered for Carly after all. He sighed and pressed Julia's name instead.

"Hi Noah," Julia said loudly over the noise of the boat. "What's going on? You'll have to speak up because we're on the patrol boat and it's hard to hear."

"I, uh, was looking for your sister but I don't have her number," he replied. "I figured she was probably with you, like usual. Is she?"

Julia laughed. "She's right here. I'll close my ears although I probably won't be able to hear anything she says anyway." Julia handed the phone to Carly while giving her a knowing look.

"Hi, Noah ...What did you say?...Yeah, she can be a pain sometimes ... Well, right now we're on our way to Road Town with Drew—I mean Chief Hawke." Carly laughed. "No, he's not taking us to jail. What's up?"

Carly put the phone on mute and said to Julia, "He wants to know if it's okay for him to go to the bed-and-breakfast and wait for us. He's getting a ride into town with one of the security guys because they had a late schedule of filming today."

Julia frowned. "Well, obviously he can't do that with Monique there." She turned to Drew and asked, "Is there some way that Noah could help us?"

The pilot slowed the boat as they approached the Road Town harbor entrance's 5 MPH zone. Drew pursed his lips. "Ask if he knows where the police station is in town."

Noah replied that he did when Carly took him off mute and asked. She turned to Drew. "Why do you want to know?"

Drew asked Julia, "Do you two trust him?"

Julia and Carly looked at each other and nodded with a slow shrug of the shoulder thrown in. "We don't know him real well, but he hasn't given us any reason to be concerned about him. Yet," said Julia.

Noah overheard the comment and said to Carly, "I swear I'm honest. What's going on? Why are you on the patrol boat?"

Carly said, "I'll let you talk to Drew." She handed the phone to him.

Drew gave Noah instructions to be dropped off in town at his usual pub, the Sapphire, order a drink and wait fifteen minutes, then leave through the back entrance by the restrooms. An officer would drive up in an unmarked police vehicle. "Wait for him to say the password I just gave you before you get in the car. Officer Thompson will give you more information. "

"This is really cloak and dagger," exclaimed Carly while Drew talked with one of the officers on his radio phone, explaining what he'd just set up with Noah.

Julia nodded. "I wonder why he's letting Noah in on this."

RAY AND JACK watched from the darkness of a clump of trees and shrubs near the house while one man hopped out of the black SUV, engine running, and went up to a door and knocked. A moment later, two men carried a limp woman from the house and threw her into the back of the van, after which they jumped into the vehicle. It sped off, leaving a dust trail in its wake.

Ray related what they'd seen to Drew and that they were still in pursuit. "It looks like they're headed to the dock at Leverick Bay. Do you want us to intervene?" he asked, knowing he would need backup for the two-against-four scenario if they tried to make an arrest.

"Not yet. I'll call for aerial coverage from the Coast Guard.

Stay out of sight and report what you see. If we're right, and a little bit lucky, these guys will lead us to one of the boats they're using to move drugs."

"Roger. Copy that."

"I'll be standing by." Drew maneuvered the patrol boat into a slip reserved for official business.

Julia said, "You think that was Sonja, don't you?"

Drew snorted. "Yes, I do. The good news is that we can be pretty sure she's still alive."

NOAH STOOD at the bar at the Sapphire, acting as nonchalant as he could. It was more difficult than he thought it would be considering that he was used to acting in front of a movie camera. He chatted with the barmaid as he had done multiple times before during the several weeks he had been on the island. Leaning with his elbows on the bar, facing the Friday evening crowd, he scanned the faces. Most of them were familiar to him. He hadn't seen Luke since earlier in the day and wondered where he'd gone. He often hung out at this bar in his free time. Noah thought it unusual that he wasn't there for the extended happy hour on Friday evening.

He shrugged and sipped his Angel's Envy whiskey slowly, checking the door every few moments for new faces. At a quarter past the hour, he left money on the bar and casually exited through the back entrance near the men's room. An unmarked car pulled up from the back of the dark parking lot and stopped to let him in. Noah opened the door, peeked in, and said, "Copper mine." When the driver replied with the word "harmonica," Noah nodded and hopped in.

"Hi Noah," the driver said. "I'm Officer Will Thompson. You can call me 'Will.'" He turned and nodded to his passenger before driving out of the parking lot. "I'm supposed to deliver you to Antonio's home. Do you know him?"

"No, sir. What will we be doing tonight?"

"I'm not sure of the details but he and several others are monitoring the location of what we think is the main ship for a drug-running organization."

"Why are Julia and Carly with Chief Hawke?"

"He promised they could be in on the action. From a distance, of course. We don't let civilians participate in anything potentially dangerous." Officer Will checked the time. "They should be leaving from Road Town any minute now."

Noah chuckled. "Too bad we can't trade places. I'd love to be in the middle of things myself."

"Chief says we need you on land. Antonio could use your help."

JACK AND RAY followed the black SUV along Leverick Bay Road, staying back as far as possible while still being able to observe whether it pulled off on another side road. It finally stopped in a small parking lot next to a pier where a dozen boats or more were tied up in the finger slips. Three men emerged from the van. Two of them manhandled the limp body and carried it down the dock to the far end where a forty-foot cabin cruiser waited. They boarded the boat themselves after transferring their load to two men with waiting hands.

The black SUV maneuvered a turn in the parking area and left.

Jack and Ray waited till the van was around the corner, then hurried toward the end of the dock. The boat was starting to pull away.

"We don't need to worry about the van. I've already run the license plate. He'll be easy to find if we need them," said Ray to Jack. "Can you see any identifying marks on that boat with the binoculars?"

"I can see some letters on the side but no real name. I think the letters are 'DMDT.'" He handed the field glasses to Ray. "That's a crazy boat name. What do you think it means?"

CHAPTER
TWENTY-SEVEN

Sonja opened her eyes to the roar of a powerboat and quickly realized that she was on it and that it was moving. She was lying with her hands tied behind her back on some sort of bench in a cabin. The boat's movements caused her to roll back and forth. It was difficult without the use of her hands and arms, but she finally struggled to a sitting position. She could see darkness through the portholes. Her head pounded with a thundering headache and her mouth was parched. She looked around for water but didn't see anything handy—not that she could get it to her mouth anyway with her hands secured so tightly.

She pushed herself to a standing position, grateful that her legs were free and strong from her dancing, and lurched across the small room to the door. Managing even that was a small feat in itself with the boat rocking from side to side as it sped through the water. She turned her back to the door and tried the handle, just in case. Locked. She kicked the door with her foot as hard as she could, again and again. When no one came to her rescue after two or three minutes, she kicked it again even harder.

She searched the cabin for something that would make noise but didn't find anything useful. Pillows and blankets weren't going to cut it. She sat down in disgust and waited until she figured at least five minutes had passed, then got up once more to kick the wooden door. Just as she was ready to swing her leg as hard as she could, the door opened and knocked her over. She fell with a thud to the hard floor, her bound arms useless to catch herself.

"I need a drink of water, you goon," she yelled at the person in the doorway as she struggled to get to a sitting position on the floor.

"Sonja, it's me, Luke. Let me help you up."

Sonja's jaw dropped and she turned around at the sound of Luke's voice. "What are you doing here? Why am I on this boat? Where are you taking me?"

Luke helped her onto her feet, then onto the bench. He smiled and put his fingers to his lips, then whispered, "It's a long story that I can't tell you right now. I promise I won't let anyone hurt you, but I have to let you stay in here for now." He reached into a cupboard, pulled out a water bottle, and opened it. He held it for her while she guzzled half of it down. He put his arm around her and held her close for a moment.

"What's going on, Luke?" Sonja said, melting into him. "I'm scared."

"I know. I'm going to untie your hands, but you need to pretend that they're still bound if anyone else comes in here. I'll try to keep them away from this cabin."

"Where are we going?"

"I'm really not sure. The captain won't reveal the destination until we get further out to sea."

"Is Monique on the boat, too?"

"No. We haven't found her since she escaped. Boss is really mad about that. So, I can't let you get away like she did."

"Am I going to die like that girl on the beach?" Sonja felt tears leak from her eyes.

Luke squeezed her arm. "No. I won't let that happen. I have to leave now so Sammy doesn't miss me, but I'll be back."

Sonja watched tearfully as Luke left and pulled the door closed behind him. She heard the latch lock with finality.

RITA OPENED the door to Antonio's office where he and Monique were watching several boats on the screen. He was explaining the Automatic Identification System, or AIS, which was used to identify all vessels on the world's waterways. Other boaters, or anyone using the system online, could tell if a blip on their navigation system was a tugboat pulling a barge, or a container ship, or even a ferry, for example.

"That's really cool," said Monique. "Do all boats and ships use this system?"

"No," said Antonio. "Generally, it's used by any honest company, but I wouldn't expect our bad boys out there to be identifying themselves." He looked to see who had entered the room. "Monique, we have company."

Noah stood in the doorway and stared blankly at Monique, then at Antonio. "I thought you hadn't found her yet," he was finally able to say. He took the three steps across the room and gave her shoulder a squeeze. "I'm so glad to see you."

"Hi, Noah," Monique said quietly. "Antonio's been teaching me some things. I might want to join the Coast Guard when I grow up." She smiled and turned back to the computer screen. "What's that boat, Antonio?" She pointed to a new blip on the western edge of the navigation screen view. "It doesn't have a number on it."

"Good observation, young lady." Antonio patted her on the back. "Let's see if we can learn anything more about it." He handed her a manual with notations and asked her to look through the list to see if she could match the new sighting with any of the markers.

Antonio stood. He was several inches taller than Noah and solidly built. "You must be the Noah I've been hearing about." He offered a hand. "Welcome. Monique is a quick study. Do you know anything about AIS?"

Noah returned the gesture and reddened. "No, sir, I mean, I know a little about it but not really very much." He turned his head away quickly when he noticed the doubtful look crossing Antonio's face.

"Okay, then." Antonio pulled up a third chair for Noah and pointed to it. "I'll continue the explanation as if you were a novice."

"Yes, sir," said Noah, sitting down on the other side of Monique, who sneaked a little smile at him.

"As I told Monique, the AIS, or Automatic Identification System, is used to keep track of marine vessels in the world's waterways. More than a half million boats have it installed. In fact, it's required for any boat that has gross tonnage of 300 or more, and for all passenger boats, regardless of size."

"Is it legal to require it for all those boats?" asked Noah. "Shouldn't it be voluntary instead?"

"It's a matter of safety for the most part. Ship captains use it to prevent their boats from running into each other. And it's free to use even if you don't have AIS installed on your own boat. For example, a pleasure boat sailing here in the Caribbean can use it to see if there are any major vessels in its path. This is especially useful at night when it's harder to see other boats and ships. Or in foul weather, which can creep up very quickly. Shipping companies use it to track movement of their ships around the world."

"It reminds me of the locator in my cell phone," said Monique. "Mom worries less about me when she knows I have my phone with me, and she can look to see where I am."

"Seems like spying to me," said Noah.

"Hmm," said Antonio. "That sounds like something that a person with something to hide would say." He looked at Noah with narrowed eyes.

Noah leaned away and raised his hands. "Just saying. Hey, I'm a Millennial. That's how we think."

Antonio nodded and explained further. "Small private vessels may or may not have an AIS number. It's optional, and even then, the transmitter can be turned off, although that would be illegal if a vessel is required to be registered."

"Antonio," said Monique, "how do the big boats stay away from the little boats? If they don't have this system, I mean."

"Many, if not most, boats employ some form of radar primarily for safety so other boats can detect them on the water. It's useful in fog or bad weather, particularly. So even if a thirty-foot sailboat, for example, doesn't use AIS, we can still 'see' it with sophisticated radar, provided it's within the range of the unit being used."

"I think I kinda understand," said Monique. "But not really."

Antonio chuckled. "There's another rule in the boating world that also covers that. The smaller or more maneuverable vessel is required to stay out of the way of the bigger one. So a powerboat that can move and change its course faster has to avoid a slower-moving sailboat. On the roads, it's like a car staying out of the way of a big semi-truck. That truck can't stop as quickly, so a car has to yield the right of way to avoid collision." He smiled at Monique, who had a blank look on her face.

"What's a semi-truck?"

Antonio and Noah looked at each other and laughed when they realized there were no such things on the narrow roads of Virgin Gorda. Antonio pulled up an image of a semi online instead.

"I would definitely stay away from one of those," Monique announced gravely.

TWENTY-EIGHT

aving docked the police patrol boat, Drew, Julia and Carly walked down the pier to the waiting Coast Guard boat, which looked much larger than the boat they'd taken from Spanish Town even though it was only four feet longer.

Drew introduced Julia and Carly to the boat's captain, Eric, and then sat down in the co-captain's seat.

"This feels like being in a scene on *Magnum, P.I.*," said Carly.

The captain smiled at her and said, "We won't be doing any of that aerobatic maneuvering on the water, I'm afraid. I hope you won't be disappointed. Welcome aboard." He checked his navigational instruments and talked on the microphone for a few seconds. He nodded at Drew and asked, "Ready?"

"Let's go find these guys."

"The last sighting at Leverick Bay suggested that our target was heading north and west from the docks there," said Drew.

"The mega yacht was observed heading westerly along the north side of Anegada, according to Antonio."

Julia's ears perked up. "*Our* Antonio?"

Drew turned his head and nodded. "He's one of our land-based trackers. He's good, too."

Eric said, "We're going to try to find that smaller boat and see if we can tell if and where it's going to intercept that yacht being tracked by Antonio's group. Ladies, you'll find night-vision binoculars in the pockets in front of you. Watch for a boat about forty to fifty feet long, moving east to west. Report anything you see, and we'll ask Antonio to check it out further."

"Yes, sir," said Julia, with Carly nodding.

Drew was using another pair of powerful night-vision binoculars to scan the horizon. "Has Bluebird One spotted the mega yacht recently?"

Eric said, "They've got a suspicious yacht in view. It doesn't have AIS activated, although we suspect a boat that size has it installed, just not turned on."

"How big is it?" asked Drew.

"It's a two-hundred-footer."

Drew whistled. "Do you know anything else about it?"

Eric shook his head. "Our boys in the boats haven't gotten close enough to get any other details. This yacht cruises just outside our usual jurisdiction, which adds to our suspicion that it's trying to avoid detection and the authorities."

"I see a boat moving off to our right," said Julia. "It looks like it's heading toward the north side of Tortola."

Drew focused his attention on the boat. "That's one of the fishing boats from Road Town," he said after a moment. "I'm pretty sure he's not who we're after. Good eye, though, Julia."

Julia sighed. "It's hard to tell who's who down here on the water."

Eric said, "Our chopper pilots spend so many hours in the air they can tell the regulars from the visitors, and the fishing boats from the pleasure boats, and so on. Unfortunately, the drug runners typically use ordinary but fast yachts that are normal in every way on the outside. Many of them have been stolen from another area and relocated here where nobody knows the boat."

"Most of the time we stumble onto them purely by luck and chance," said Drew. "Like when you took the video of those two boats at Mountain Trunk Bay. We can put that up on our watch list and might get lucky enough to intercept them and interrupt somebody's drug circuit."

"I had no idea it was that difficult to catch these guys," said Julia, "but there's a lot of water and territory to cover out here."

"And that makes a lot of places for them to hide," added Carly.

Monique diligently checked each blip against the master list that Antonio had given her. She started to recognize patterns of boat behavior, such as speed, direction of travel, and how far offshore it was. She looked up the AIS numbers that showed up and noted each of them in the spreadsheet Antonio had given her. The kitty, Malla, purred contentedly in her lap. When she saw a boat without an AIS designation, she noted its characteristics in the notebook and pointed it out to Antonio.

"Antonio," she asked, "is there a way to tell if this blip is one of the ones that should have an AIS number? It seems bigger than a lot of the other ones I've seen."

Antonio and Noah examined the vessel on the screen. It

was almost due west of Anegada, the northernmost large island of the British Virgin Isles.

"I've noted traffic using that route several times over the last few months," said Antonio. "I can't be sure it's the same vessel, but if it is, it will head southwest toward Puerto Rico, staying a fair distance north of Tortola."

"Is that normal behavior?" Noah asked. "Do you have any idea who it is?"

"Given Julia's observations of an interaction between that yacht and a powerboat earlier today at Mountain Trunk Bay, and the comments that Monique overheard about her kidnappers meeting the 'big boat' tonight, I have a hunch this might be one of the drug-running ships doing business between the United States and Puerto Rico and Venezuela."

"If you think that's what it is, why hasn't it been stopped before?" Noah asked point-blank.

"The Coast Guard has to have enough evidence to stop and search a vessel and generally can only do so within their jurisdiction. These guys are clever and stay out of bounds for the most part. Most of them are using yachts they've commandeered from innocent citizens, and they ditch them after a few runs to avoid suspicion from multiple uses. They know we're watching."

"Who's 'we'?"

Antonio looked up and smiled. "People like me."

Noah's eyes narrowed at Antonio. "You're not going to tell me who you really are, are you?"

"Not yet. I've got work to do." He called the command station and reported the location of the unidentified vessel. He then turned to Monique. "What else have you found, young lady?"

∾

JULIA AND CARLY dutifully scanned the water around them in all directions. After a few minutes of observations, Julia realized that she was able to gauge the speed of the slower-moving boats more easily than before and could identify the clunkier fishing boats from sleeker yachts and other powerboats and sailboats. A fast-moving powerboat coming from the east caught her attention because it was moving decidedly faster than any other traffic in her visual field.

"Drew," she said, "check out the boat ahead that's heading north-northwest." She looked up with eyes wide. "He's in a big hurry. I think it's a powerboat by its shape."

After verifying Julia's observation, Drew called Antonio and asked him if they could detect the boat on their radar.

"Monique and I are on it. I'll call you back in a few," Antonio replied.

Eric stayed within visual range of the boat, making a giant figure eight in the water as they waited for a call from Antonio.

A few minutes later Drew's phone lit up. "What did you find?"

"We see the boat," said Antonio. "It's heading northwest at about 290 degrees as Julia mentioned, and if it stays on its current course, will intersect the path with that big yacht at about 18 degrees north and 65 degrees west. So far, they're both staying on a straight course. I've relayed this information to Max at the command post already. He'll inform the Coast Guard cutter's captain."

"Thanks, Antonio. Over."

Drew called the command center and reported his location.

"Antonio said he talked to Max," said Julia. "Is he the same Max who rescued Carly and me from Dead Chest Island?"

"Yes, indeed, Miss Julia. He and Ben are retired coast

guardsmen who now live on Tortola. They volunteer their services for this kind of activity."

"No wonder he knew how to handle that boat so well," said Julia.

"Yes," said Drew. "You were in good hands." To Eric he said, "The Commander wants us to stay on the tail of the powerboat you spotted. The Coast Guard chopper is heading to the location of the bigger yacht."

"Won't they get suspicious if we stay right near them?" asked Carly.

"We'll move around so it looks like we're doing routine surveillance," said Drew. "The local boaters know we're on the water on a regular basis, ready to help." He chuckled. "But I like to make the bad dudes nervous and let them think I'm onto them."

Julia asked, "But you can't really do anything, can you?"

"Not directly, but they know the Coast Guard might show up anytime and that's what makes them worry if they have anything to hide. Currently, we have a cutter in the water a mile or so from the ship that Antonio and his buddies are watching. It looks like a 200-foot yacht according to what they're seeing on radar. We're far enough away that we're not likely to be detected unless someone is pointing their radar system directly at us. Anyway, our men will move in once we or the chopper can confirm that these two boats are approaching each other. In the meantime, we'll all stay out of sight."

"But it's dark out," said Julia. "Wouldn't the boat we're tracking notice our lights?"

"Eric is being careful to stay far enough away from the powerboat to not arouse undue suspicion. We can track him with radar even if we can't put our actual eyes on him. That's what Antonio and Monique are doing from the ground."

"There are a lot of moving parts out here," said Julia. "I hope nothing goes wrong."

CHAPTER

TWENTY-NINE

Drew's phone buzzed with an incoming text message. He frowned when he saw the attached photo. "Julia, could this be one of the actors from that pirate movie? He looks familiar from when we interviewed the cast and film crew after Monique disappeared." He handed her the phone.

"It sure looks like Noah, although it's quite blurry. Carly, what do you think?" Julia asked as she passed the phone to her sister.

Carly scrutinized the hazy image before saying, "I agree that it could be Noah. But I think it looks more like Luke. They really do look a lot alike except for the eyes, which I can't see very well in this picture." She handed the phone back to Drew. "Where was this taken? Do you know?"

Drew perused the message that had accompanied the photo. "Lenny said this email just came in from an antiquities shop in San Juan. They'd gotten the memo we'd sent out earlier in the week and found this in their security footage.

Apparently, they always take photos of this kind of interaction, just in case."

"What kind of interaction?" asked Julia.

"Any time someone comes in with something valuable, such as jewelry or supposed pirate treasure, this store documents the transaction via video," said Drew. "I'm guessing they've been burned in the past and this is their way of protecting themselves against the law or libel or claims by crazies."

"This means that Noah must be in on the treasure looting and kidnapping of Monique, after all," said Julia.

"Or Luke," said Carly.

"Isn't Noah at Antonio's right now with Monique?" asked Julia.

Drew nodded grimly. "And I arranged for him to be there. I'll call Ray and let him know we have a new situation."

SONJA SHIVERED in the cabin despite the fact that the temperature was in the seventies. Evenings seemed cooler in the Caribbean after the sun went down despite what the thermometer might say. She was frightened despite Luke's reassurances that she would be okay. She wasn't sure she could trust him, knowing there had to be other men on the boat. He was almost certainly outnumbered. She jumped at the sound of footsteps outside the door and hurried to move to the corner of the settee, where she held her hands behind her as if they were still tied.

One of the men she'd seen acting as a security guard on the pirate movie set unlatched the door from the outside and looked around inside the room. "Is Luke in here?" he asked.

Sonja shook her head. "I haven't seen him. No one's in here

besides me."

"Boss is looking for him. Tell him if you see him." He turned and left the room, firmly pulling the latch closed.

Sonja let out her breath, grateful he hadn't come any closer. She was worried for herself, as well as for Luke. She wished she'd never gone to the movie set and that everything would go back to how it was before. She even missed the three little boys at the foster home, even though they were little spitfires when Mrs. Reynolds wasn't around. She had been worrying because she was going to age out of the foster system in another year and didn't know what would happen to her. She'd even tolerate the little demons if she could stay in a safe home. She felt tears again. All she had wanted was a real boyfriend and maybe a little excitement in her life, but this was more than she'd counted on.

RITA HUMMED to herself as she went to answer the door. She was happy that Monique seemed to enjoy helping her bake and learning about Antonio's marine tracking system. She pulled it open and did a double take. A stranger faced her, a gun in his hand pointed at her. She only managed a gasp before the stocky man grabbed her arm and pulled her around in front of his chest. The gun's barrel pressed hard on her rib cage.

"Where is Noah?" he asked with a rough voice. "My guy said he followed him here earlier."

Rita nodded slowly and tilted her head toward the door where Antonio, Monique and Noah were monitoring the computer. "In there with my husband," she said softly.

"Walk slowly and don't do anything foolish." The man pushed her ahead of him, his free hand gripping her arm tightly, across the room. "Open the door quietly. Tell your husband he has company."

Rita opened the door as she was instructed and said, "Tony, we have a visitor."

Antonio turned to see his wife's ashen face, one arm bent back, a stranger's glare directly behind her, scanning the room. Monique shrieked and ran to Rita, who put her other arm protectively around her shoulders. She whispered in her ear. Monique nodded and stood stock still where she was, pressing her tiny body into Rita.

Noah crossed the small room in three steps. "It's about time you got here, Brock. The Coast Guard has a lock on the Queen ship and is monitoring DMDT." He pulled a knife from his boot.

Monique asked, "What's DMDT?"

Brock scoffed. "It's the boat's name ... *Dead Men Don't Talk.*"

Monique shivered.

Antonio stood and moved a few inches to his left. "What now, Brock? How are you going to fight the Coast Guard?"

Brock laughed. "Oh, I think having a couple of hostages will give me an advantage. I know they don't like to leave dead bodies around, especially children." He looked sideways at Monique with a sneer on his face.

Antonio had slowly inched toward the end of his computer table while Brock talked. When Rita winked at him, Antonio yelled, "*Now,*" and Rita stomped on Brock's instep. She whirled around when he loosened his grip on her arm and used a karate chop on Brock's gun arm. Brock howled and dropped his gun, startling Noah, who fumbled with his knife and scrambled to retrieve it. Antonio lunged at Noah, keeping his head and body low. Monique jumped behind Rita to kick Brock in the back of his knee. Rita kicked Brock's gun away while

Antonio snatched up Noah's knife and held it against Noah's ribs. Noah raised his hands. Rita twisted Brock's arm behind him while he yowled, hobbling on his injured leg.

At that moment Ray and Jack burst into the room, surveyed the situation, and stood for a moment with mouths open.

"I'm not sure you need us," said Ray. "What's the situation here?"

Antonio nodded at Noah. "He's the movie star, Noah Langdon. The other guy is Brock Hughes, the director of the movie being filmed here on the island. They obviously also have other roles they're playing that have nothing to do with the movies. You can have them."

"Okay, gentlemen," said Jack as he and Ray handcuffed Noah and Brock. "You can watch some real pirate movies in jail."

"I guess you guys didn't know Rita has her black belt in karate," Antonio said as Noah and Brock were escorted out the door. "You really shouldn't mess with her."

ANTONIO CONTACTED Drew to apprise him of the situation and to report the name of the newly identified boat, *Dead Men Don't Talk.* "That other boat Julia saw has veered off to the north, so I don't think it's the one we want."

"Are you telling me that Noah and Brock are in on this?" Drew asked Antonio.

"It looks that way, Drew. But I don't think either of them is the leader of the ring. They're underlings of some sort."

"Did you get any other names out of them?"

"Not while they were here. Ray and Jack showed up not long after Brock burst in, so I didn't have time to get anything else out of them."

"That's too bad," said Drew, snorting. "Maybe Ray or Jack learned something."

"We can only hope."

"Well, let me know when you find that damn powerboat."

DREW TURNED to Julia and Carly, who sat with him in the boat's cockpit. "I suppose you heard most of that."

"I can't believe Noah is a bad guy," Carly wailed. "I want a do-over."

Julia shook her head. "I would believe it of Luke, but not Noah. There's got to be more to the story. We still have to find Sonja. Maybe Noah will help with that."

"Only if he knows something. That would redeem him a little bit, I suppose," said Carly.

The sisters and Drew scanned the dark water around them silently as the police boat continued its search for the elusive powerboat. A long five minutes passed without sighting anything remotely resembling a forty-foot boat, power-type or otherwise.

Julia was the first to spot a light moving rapidly across the water from an easterly direction. She watched it for about a minute before saying anything. "Drew, check the water to our right. I'm seeing a boat there that's really got the pedal to the metal. I can't tell if it's the right size, but it's heading north-west. It doesn't look like a fishing boat to me, at least not at that speed."

Drew peered through his binoculars and nodded. "Could be the one. Eric, will you please send our coordinates to Antonio and see if he can identify it on his screen?"

"Yes, sir." Eric quickly relayed the information.

THIRTY

L enny, Drew's Assistant Police Chief, sat with Ray and Jack in the conference room at the police station.

"Did either Noah or Brock say anything helpful?" Lenny asked the two officers.

"Brock—Mr. Hughes, the director, the stubby guy—wants to talk to an attorney first," said Ray. "He clammed up right away."

"Okay," said Lenny. "He can sit in jail over the weekend unless he has some kind of magic pull to get somebody to come here before Monday. What about the handsome dude?"

Jack snickered. "He kept saying we should remember his name, Noah Langdon. I guess he expects to be famous someday."

"He's not going to be making movies if he's in jail," said Lenny. "Did he say anything about what these guys are up to?"

"Not exactly," said Jack, "but he said something like, 'these amateurs don't know anything about shooting a movie and less about pawning jewelry.'"

Ray added, "I didn't get the impression *he* knows much

about running drugs and jewelry either. It's like it's all about making a movie."

Lenny scoffed. "Did he think Brock was doing a publicity stunt or something?"

Jack shrugged. "Noah may be a good-looking guy as far as women go, but I don't think he's very smart."

"So they're most likely working for someone else," said Lenny. "Maybe we'll be able to crack the ring when the Coast Guard catches up with that oversized yacht."

LUKE PACED BACK and forth on the flying bridge of the powerboat, looking out the windshield all the while for signs of the Boss's ship. "What's the ETA for the hookup with the *Queen*?" he asked the boat's captain.

Sammy was at the wheel, pushing the cabin cruiser at its maximum speed despite the rough water, which was making the ride bumpier than usual. "We should be meeting in the next twenty minutes unless something else happens. I've had to make up for the time we lost when we had to stop to pick up that girl from Hank and Dude." He scoffed. "Should have left her behind. That girl has been nothing but trouble since she's been aboard, but Boss wanted us to bring at least one of the dancers."

"Why does he want one of the dancers?"

Sammy gave Luke a knowing look. "Why do you think? At the very least he might be able to use her as collateral when we go back to Venezuela after the run to Miami, if she's pretty enough."

"She's pretty, but she's just a teenager."

"He likes 'em young. They're more valuable as bargaining chips."

Luke felt his stomach lurch. His mind raced as he considered how he could keep Sonja safe. But would she ever forgive him, even if he were able to get her out of this mess?

"What's going to happen when we meet up with the mother ship?" Luke asked.

"We'll transfer the drugs and the girl once we meet them, and then head back to Virgin Gorda. Oh, yeah. Boss wants you to do the whole run with them this time."

"Me? Why? I'm not ready to go that far yet."

"Too bad. Boss makes the rules. You don't want him to think you're a liability, right?" Sammy gave Luke a sideways look. "You'll be going, like it or not." Sammy's eyes held a cold glint as deadly as the sharp edge of a knife, and Luke turned away to look out at the sea.

ANTONIO AND MONIQUE huddled in front of the computer monitor using the coordinate numbers that Eric had given them to plot the course of *Dead Men Don't Talk.* They were able to eliminate three vessels from consideration because their AIS tags identified them as two tankers and a cruise ship. The fourth vessel did not have an AIS tag and was moving at a fast clip, according to the satellite radar. And it was in the correct field to be the boat that Julia had spotted.

"Let's give Drew a call," said Antonio. "Okay, Monique?"

She nodded. "They need to rescue Sonja, just like they rescued me."

"Yes, she's our first priority." Antonio hugged her briefly, then picked up the phone. "Drew, I'd put money on that unidentified boat being the one that Ray and Jack saw leaving Leverick Bay. Coordinates put it about twenty minutes away from the big boat that we think is the main drug-running ship."

"Thanks. We'll stay on its tail. Eric says we should have enough fuel to stay out here 'til it's over."

"Roger that."

"Are Julia and Carly safe with Drew and that pilot guy?" asked Monique. "What happens if their boat *does* run out of fuel?"

Antonio smiled kindly. "Eric is keeping an eye on that. And if necessary, they can float out there for a while and the Coast Guard will rescue them."

"I still hope they don't run out of fuel."

"That makes two of us."

THE CAPTAIN of the *Queen Bee* sat in the pilot's chair and scanned the horizon every few minutes, as was his habit when he was on the water. He was typically on full alert when he was in this part of the Caribbean, but even more so when he had valuable cargo on board, as he did for this run. He had gotten a little too close to a Coast Guard cutter on his last trip and didn't want to repeat the experience.

He had tried to warn the Boss that he needed to ditch this yacht, despite its usefulness, and commandeer another one. Stolen yachts were only good for so long before the authorities got suspicious. He was worried that one of the monitoring agencies was going to notice his frequent runs to and from Venezuela and have the Coast Guard stop him for a search. He usually kept out of the island waters that were under the Coast Guard jurisdiction of either the United States or United Kingdom, but even that maneuver could eventually trigger someone's antennae. No place on the water was entirely safe for drug traffickers. Today's sophisticated radar systems were getting harder to evade.

The captain heard a knock on the door and turned to see his boss coming to join him.

"Hello, Señor Pedro," said Captain Welch. "We should be meeting the other boat in the next fifteen minutes."

"Have you noticed anything worrisome out on the water tonight?" Señor Pedro glanced through the windows at the water. The moon threw its long stream of light almost parallel to the boat's path.

"Nothing at all," the captain replied. "No Coast Guard cutters, for sure. I haven't seen nothin' but big shippers and cruise ships out there tonight." He pointed at the navigation system's monitor. "Everything out here matches up with the usual traffic."

"Very good. Then we should be safe once we get the rest of our goods on board and can travel farther away from the islands."

"Yes, sir."

THIRTY-ONE

L uke leaned on the starboard rail of the powerboat. There were three other men on the boat: Sammy, who was driving, Dude, and the security guy named Manuel who always seemed to have a harmonica on him. Luke chuckled to himself. That guy seriously needed lessons. He walked toward the stern, making note of their current positions. Sammy was at the wheel, of course, and was talking to Dude. Luke moved closer to the bridge so he could hear the conversation. He heard Sammy say, "We'll pull up port to port. Get the bumpers out and be ready to toss them between us and *Queen Bee*. Manuel can manage the bowline and Luke can take the stern. Are the satchels ready to transfer?"

Luke assumed Manuel was in the main salon as he hadn't seen him anywhere else when he circled the boat. He knew he would have to work quickly for his plan to work. It was convenient that Sammy had assigned him to the stern for the rendezvous. He stepped into the cockpit and grabbed a couple of boat cushions from under the settee's bench seat. He walked quickly to the cabin where Sonja was being held, unlocked and opened the door from the outside, and went inside.

"Luke!" Sonja got up to put her arms around him. "What's going on? How much longer before we get to wherever we're going?"

He put his fingers to his lips and whispered, "I'm going to set these cushions on fire on the top deck to create a diversion. I'll come back here to get you and we are going to run to the Zodiac at the back of the boat. I'll lower it into the water with the hydraulic system and we'll climb in. That will take a couple of minutes, but I think we'll have enough time while the other guys deal with the fire. It'll take them a little longer because I hid the fire extinguishers."

Sonja managed a little snicker. "Then what? We're in the middle of nowhere out here."

"Hang on to these flares." He handed her two skinny red sticks. "Once we're far enough from the boat we'll set them off and hope someone sees them. Can you do that?"

Sonja nodded, eyes wide.

"I'll be back in five minutes. Stand right by the door and be ready to run out." He kissed her quickly and left the room.

Luke didn't see anyone when he exited. His heart raced as he hurried to the upper deck, laid the cushions in the center of the space, then lit them with a cigarette lighter. Once he was sure they had caught fire and were burning, he scooted down the ladder to the main deck and rescued Sonja.

They hurried to the stern where the Zodiac was suspended. He instructed Sonja to stand on the platform at water level while he released the davit and lowered the boat. Once it was in the water, they both jumped in. He started the motor and they sped off. Luke wasn't a boater but guessed that the closest land was to the south. He looked at the moon—still high in the sky in the west—to get his bearings and gunned the motor, heading in what he hoped was the correct direction.

Luke and Sonja had motored several hundred yards away from *Dead Men Don't Talk* when they heard screams from Dude and Manuel, who had noticed first smoke, then fire. Luke had worried that Sammy would come after him when he realized what had happened but figured getting the cocaine and fentanyl to the *Queen Bee* was much more valuable than coming after the two of them.

Luke breathed a big sigh of relief when the powerboat maintained its course to meet Boss and deliver its cargo. He put his free arm around a shivering Sonja and hugged her. "Now we only have to worry about how much gas we have. Let's let them get a little farther away before we set off a flare."

JULIA AND CARLY continued to scan the water with the powerful binoculars. Julia was scanning the starboard side and Carly was covering the port side. Julia noticed a light appear suddenly in the direction of the boat she'd seen earlier. The light persisted. She handed the field glasses to Drew. "What's that light off to our right? It just popped up."

While they watched, trying to figure out the source of the light, Julia spotted a streak of light going into the sky. Having used a flare gun a few days before, she recognized the arc of the light's path. "Drew! I see a flare between us and that light!"

"I see it too," he replied. "Eric, let's head toward that flare. Someone's in trouble."

It was a long three minutes before the patrol boat neared the Zodiac. Sonja and Luke were yelling, "Help! Help!" as Eric slowed down to avoid swamping the smaller boat. Drew leaned out over the rail and threw a line over the water which

Luke caught and secured to the dinghy. He attached a second line to the Zodiac's stern while Drew lowered the bigger boat's ladder over the side.

Luke helped Sonja climb into the patrol boat, then followed her.

Sonja burst into sobs when Drew handed her a blanket. Julia and Carly hugged her tightly.

"We're so glad to find you," said Julia.

Luke answered, "Thank you! I don't know if I could have found land by myself." Luke wrapped himself in the blanket offered by Eric. "We just got away from that yacht with the fire. They've got drugs onboard, if you didn't know already. They're going to meet the *Queen Bee* in about fifteen minutes."

"I'll radio the Coast Guard," said Eric. "They'll take over now that they have enough evidence to go aboard and search the boat." He turned to Luke. "Thank you, uh—what was your name?"

"Luke. Luke Hughes."

THIRTY-TWO

I t was very late and the stars were bright. Drew, Julia and Carly stood at the prow of the twenty-eight-foot TP Marine RIB as it pulled into the harbor of Spanish Town back on Virgin Gorda. Despite the midnight hour, a welcoming committee of Antonio and Rita with Monique and her parents —her mom holding the kitty, Malla—plus Teresa Reynolds and her three sons stood at the end of the pier. They were all smiles and tears as they waved exuberantly and jumped up and down.

A jubilant Sonja jumped off the boat and ran to Teresa, who sobbed and hugged her. The three brothers shrieked and joined in the hug. After a minute or so, Sonja broke off and hugged a tearful Monique.

Julia and Carly walked up to Teresa and celebrated Sonja's rescue with her, then went over to meet Monique's parents. Although the Duniecs had known for a couple of days that their daughter was safe, they were ecstatic that they finally got to see her and hold her and talk with her. And to thank Julia and Carly personally.

Julia and Carly stood with Rita and Antonio while Ray Townsend walked to the patrol boat, where Drew emerged with a remorseful Luke, now in handcuffs.

Luke lowered his head as he walked down the pier. He mumbled a quiet "I'm so sorry" to Teresa and Sonja when he passed them. He avoided looking directly at Julia and Carly on his way to the police car.

JULIA AND CARLY drove back to the inn with Antonio and Rita, where the four of them watched on the monitors to see the final moments of the Coast Guard's interception of *Dead Men Don't Talk.* The drug boat and the *Reef Shark* were side-by-side blips on the monitor screen. Julia wished she could see what was going on in livestream but had to be satisfied with Antonio's commentary of the process. He explained that the U.S. Coast Guard crewmen would have boarded the drug boat, arrested everybody, and then would take both boats back to San Juan. Once there, they would remove and confiscate any drugs that were found.

He told them of a major drug seizure of thirty-eight million dollars' worth of cocaine (1,375 kilos) eighteen months earlier, and a recovery only a few months ago of 1,700 kilos worth fifty-one million dollars near Anegada. "This is a huge business. Occasionally we get lucky, as we did with this bust thanks to you two, but there are other major players out there with multiple boats. We simply can't catch them all."

Saturday morning seemed to arrive early after the late-night adventure. The smell of bacon and eggs and cinnamon toast wafted into the girls' room.

Julia opened her eyes and said, "I can't sleep with that delicious smell. And I'm hungry."

"I need a triple-shot espresso," said Carly.

The sisters got ready in record time and after devouring the platters of food, they sat around the breakfast table with Antonio and Rita. The mood was a mix of happiness that Sonja had been rescued and sadness that both Noah and Luke appeared to be implicated in the illegal activities of Brock and his gang.

"I'm blown away that Luke is Brock's son," said Carly. "Why would he let himself be involved in something like this?"

"Maybe Brock was holding him hostage, so to speak, and forcing him to solicit the girls that the drug boss wanted for his business," said Julia. "Luke went along with it until he met Sonja and realized he didn't want her to be involved in the drug business. And neither did he."

"And finally had the courage to stand up to his dad?" said Carly.

"Exactly," said Antonio. "He had already contacted a federal agent about his father and was planning to turn State's witness even before he met Sonja. I doubt he'll have to serve any jail time after sharing what he knows."

"And Noah?" asked Rita. "What's his gig?"

"Drew called just before breakfast and said Noah was singing like that proverbial canary," said Julia. "He thought those jewels were real and didn't think anyone would notice if he filched a few pieces from the treasure chests and sold them on his own. He was shocked when that dealer in San Juan told him that they were very good fakes and not worth anything."

Carly laughed. "Serves him right. But I really don't understand why Brock hid the drugs in the treasure chests."

Antonio said, "I'm guessing that Brock typically threw a layer of the fake jewels in the chests on the top of the drugs when they were being transported from one place to another in case he got stopped by the police. He could open one and pull out a bauble or two of his fake pirate booty and unless someone dug deeper in the chest, no one would be the wiser."

Julia said, "Maybe he had a map for where his movie treasure chests and the drug chests were supposed to be buried and someone made a mistake and buried his drug chests on the wrong beach."

"Maybe the beach where Amaya saw those guys burying the bracelets is where the rest of his drugs are buried," said Carly.

"I'm sure Drew's people are already searching that beach with metal detectors," said Antonio. "They might even have Brock's map already."

Julia asked, "What if those same bracelets were what Noah tried to pawn in San Juan? And he bribed Hank and Dude to put them back for him. That sounds like something he might do."

"But was Brock the ringleader, Antonio?" asked Carly. "I don't see how he could be running drugs and shooting movies at the same time."

Antonio shook his head. "No, my little ladybirds. He was working for a man who called himself Señor Pedro. Mr. Hughes would solicit young men on the islands where he was making a movie to work as security guards on the movie set and sell a few drugs on the side. He got regular drug drops, such as the one you witnessed, that he distributed to the local drug crowd on the island where he was shooting a film. He used his son, Luke, to entice pretty girls to be in the movie. And apparently also delivered some of those girls to the *Queen Bee* for Señor Pedro's disposal."

"What about Noah?" asked Carly. "Was he in on this?"

"No, fortunately for him. He was essentially an innocent bystander who got caught up in the moment and technically didn't do anything illegal except steal a few movie props. I find it hard to believe he thought he could pawn those fake jewels as real to a dealer." Antonio shook his head and snorted.

Rita said, "But Noah pulled a knife on me."

"That, too, but I agreed with Drew that we would drop charges to get him off the island faster."

Julia's phone lit up with a call from Drew. "What's up?" She listened for a moment, then said, "I'll tell her. Thanks. Bye."

"What'd he say?" asked Carly. "You were awfully quiet."

"He's coming over with the necklace that we found with Lorena, the girl on the beach. The gemologist verified that it is an authentic seventeenth-century relic."

Rita's mouth dropped open.

THIRTY-THREE

After breakfast, Julia and Carly, Antonio and Rita walked down the sandy trail to the rock where they had originally found Lorena and the necklace. Amaya greeted them there and asked them to follow her into the forest. Rita went inside the shaman's hut with her. When they came out and stood side by side, Julia noticed a strong facial resemblance. Amaya held a small leather pouch much like the one she had shown them a few days before.

She reached in and held a silver pendant necklace in her hand. Julia and Carly gasped.

"It looks almost the same as the one we found with Lorena," said Julia.

"Yes," said Amaya. "A talented silversmith created this one from the description of the original after it was stolen from the shaman many years ago."

Rita extracted from her pocket the necklace that Drew had delivered to the house earlier, and reverently handed it to Amaya. "When Drew came to the house last evening and I saw this necklace, I knew it was the one that belonged to our people." She turned to Julia and Carly. "I would have known sooner, but I hadn't seen the photos from your finding it on the beach and it didn't register from your description."

"*Your* people?" Julia said, looking from Rita to Amaya and back to Rita. "I don't understand, but now I see the resemblance between you and Amaya."

Amaya and Rita smiled at each other, then at Julia.

Rita said, "It is true. Amaya is my sister. She was destined to be Shaman. I was allowed to follow my heart to enter the world outside our people and go to university. I wanted to pursue justice for the loss of my niece."

"So that's why you have a black belt?" asked Carly.

Rita nodded. "I worked for the CIA for many years. My chosen specialty was tracking missing persons, especially young girls. A black belt came in very handy at times when I went undercover."

"Elizabeth was my daughter," said Amaya. "She was taken from this world because of drugs. I have felt her spirit more strongly since the day you found the Arawak girl, Lorena, on the rock. I think she has been helping you find her murderer. The necklace proves it to me."

"What is it about the necklace?" asked Julia.

Amaya held in her hand the seventeenth-century pendant that Drew had delivered the previous evening. "This was a gift from a priest many generations ago to our Shaman after he saved his life. The priest had been very ill and was near death when he came to the tribe. Our shaman's medicine cured his disease. In gratitude, he gave his only valuable possession. It had been created in Portugal and he wore it as an amulet. The shaman used it for special ceremonies until it was stolen many years later. By that time it had taken on a magical aura and my grandfather didn't want the tribe to know it was gone. He spoke to a silversmith who was able to create a similar replacement, even though it couldn't be exactly duplicated. No one knew what the words on the back said because they had been written in Portuguese."

Rita said, "Now the necklace has even greater magic because it has been returned to the tribe where it belongs."

Julia said, "The priest in Spanish Town told us the inscription says, 'May God be with you always.' He isn't Portuguese himself, but the librarian in the diocesan office on St. Kitts Island was able to translate it."

"That makes sense, seeing as how it originally belonged to a Catholic priest," said Rita.

"That's right," said Amaya. "The Portuguese people came on some of the early ships and settled here on several of the islands."

"That reminds me—I didn't hear if Drew said whether he knew which of Brock's men killed Lorena," said Julia. "Antonio, do you know?"

"Brock hasn't exactly been forthcoming, but he apparently implied it was one of the locals from Road Town that he had hired for security and other purposes," he replied.

Carly asked, "What about Luke? I think he should get extra credit for saving Sonja from Señor Pedro."

"He'll be giving evidence against his father and what he knows about the drug-running operation, as I mentioned," said Antonio. "He told Drew he was ready to get out from under his father's authority and make a clean break for himself."

"Good for him," said Carly. "I'm sure it was hard to be an unwilling underling for his father's illicit businesses."

"Speaking of forthcoming, Antonio," said Julia, "I recall you ducked answering Carly's question about your occupation. You said it was 'top secret.' What did you mean?" She narrowed her eyes at him.

It was Rita's turn to chuckle. "He was originally a DEA agent who worked for me in the CIA. I taught him everything he knows." She blew her husband a kiss.

All of them laughed at Rita's revelation.

BACK AT THE BED-AND-BREAKFAST, Julia and Carly were in their bedroom finishing packing.

"How is that my clothes fit in this very same suitcase on the way here, but they refuse to cooperate for the trip back?" said Julia as she squeezed the last rolled-up t-shirt into a corner space.

"I assume that's a rhetorical question because I'm having the same problem. Good thing we didn't have time to do any serious shopping," said Carly.

"Finally," said Julia, as she managed to get her suitcase closed. "I guess it's time to drag our bags out and load the car. Are you ready?"

Carly zipped her bag and sighed. "Let's go."

Antonio and Rita were all smiles when Julia and Carly emerged. Rita gave them each a ziplock bag of goodies. "Monique and I made these. They will taste especially good when you get hungry on the plane."

"We will miss you, my little ladybirds," said Antonio as he and Rita enveloped the sisters in a group hug accompanied by a few tears.

They hugged for a moment until the doorbell rang. Sonja stood at the door with Mrs. Ritchie, the dance studio teacher.

"Come in," said Antonio, who had been the first to regain his composure. "We're getting ready to head to the ferry."

"Mrs. Ritchie said I could come to tell Julia and Carly some news," said Sonja, smiling from ear to ear as the three women came in from the patio.

"What's the news, Sonja?" asked Julia.

"I'm going to have a mom again." She looked at her teacher. "Mrs. Ritchie and her husband are going to adopt me. It's been my dream to have a real family since I was four years old." She started crying.

Mrs. Ritchie, tears in her eyes, said, "Sonja's been as close as a daughter could be since she started dancing with me. I raised two boys and they agree with my husband that they would like to have a girl in the family."

~

TEN MINUTES LATER, with tears dried and luggage in the car, Antonio whistled from the door. "Time to go, my little ladybirds."

Julia and Carly hugged Rita one last time before climbing into the car.

"Where will you two go next time for a quiet vacation?" Antonio asked as he closed the door to the back seat.

"With Julia, there is no such thing," said Carly.

"Then I'm not going to invite you to join me when I meet Josh in Seattle. His company has decided to send him to scout out the possibilities of opening a satellite office there."

"I can see the headline now: 'Dead body found on Underground Seattle Tour.' And your name will be right there."

Julia gasped. "You mean I'll be the dead body?"

"No, silly. With your luck, you'll be the tourist who finds it."

"So maybe you should go with me to keep me out of trouble." Julia grinned at her sister.

"As if."

THE END

AUTHOR'S NOTES

Virgin Gorda in the British Virgin Islands is a magical place. This story is totally fictional, other than the locations on the island itself. Any actions or portrayals of individuals, even if they are real people, are figments of my imagination.

Thank you for reading **Silent Slipper**. I hope you enjoyed it and, if you haven't already, suggest you pick up other books in the **Julia Fairchild Mystery Series.**

When you have a moment, **may I ask that you leave a review on Amazon**, Goodreads, Facebook and perhaps elsewhere you find convenient? Reviews are crucial to a book's success, and I hope for my Julia Fairchild series to have a long and successful life.

You can easily leave your review by going to my Amazon book page. Since Amazon doesn't allow review links to be posted in books, just search for **Silent Slipper**. And thank you!

If you would like to reach out for any reason, you can email me at pj@pjpetersonauthor.com. If you'd like to learn more about me and my other books, visit my website at www.pjpetersonau thor.com, where you can also sign up for my private mailing list.

Thank you,

PJ Peterson

ACKNOWLEDGMENTS

Thank you to my friends and colleagues who have inspired me, shared ideas with me, and otherwise contributed to the successful completion of yet another story in this series.

ABOUT THE AUTHOR

PJ Peterson is a retired internist who enjoyed the diagnostic part of practicing medicine as well as creating long-lasting relationships with her patients. As a child she wanted to be a doctor so she could "help people." She now volunteers at the local Free Medical Clinic to satisfy that continued need.

She loved to read from a young age and read all the Trixie Belden and Nancy Drew books she could find. It wasn't until she was an adult that she wrote anything longer than short stories and term papers.

Writing full-length mysteries now only makes sense given her early exposure to that genre. It also keeps her busy. Sprinkling in a little mystique makes it all the more fun.

Manufactured by Amazon.ca
Bolton, ON

32536514R00139